T0321316

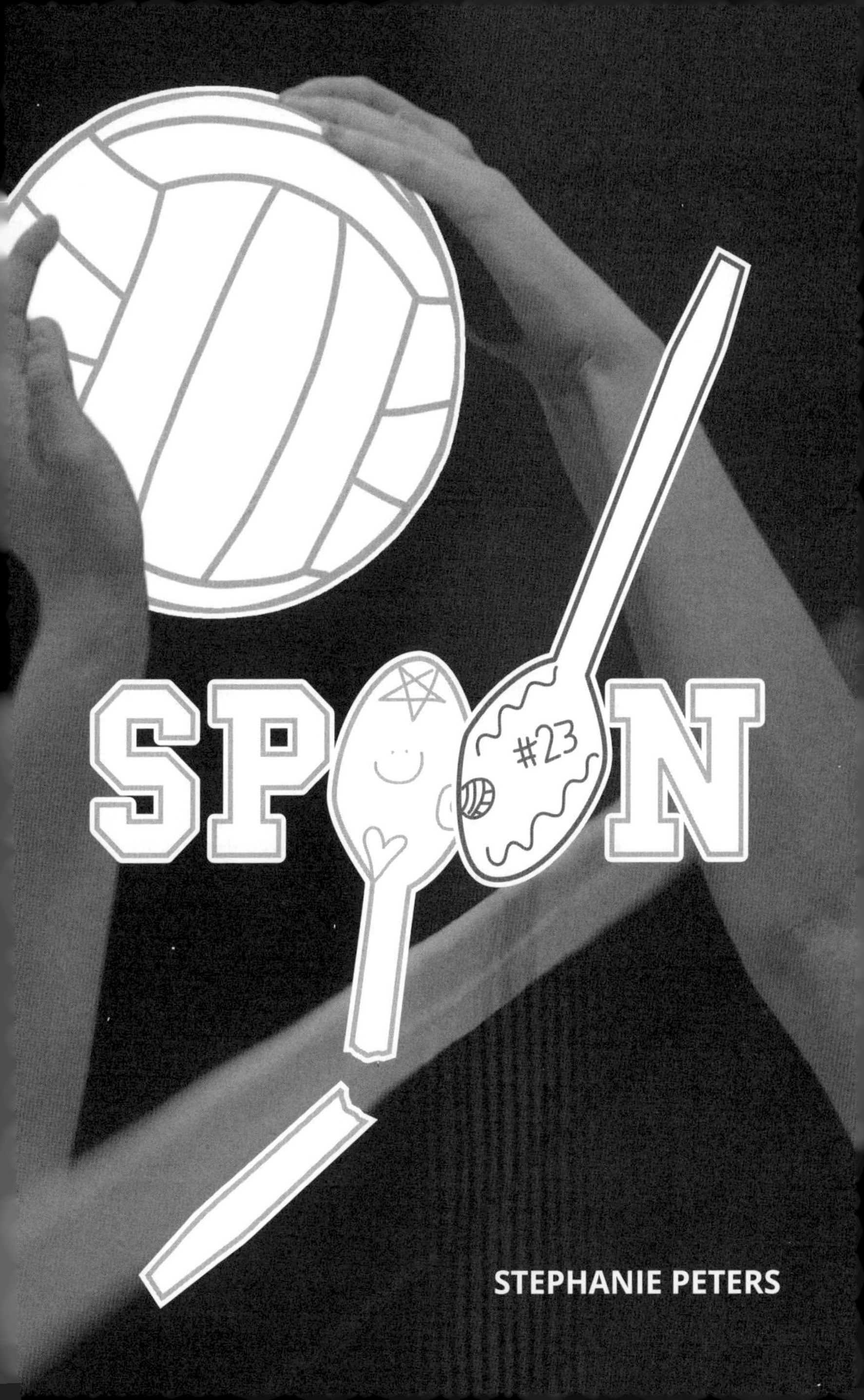
SPOON
#23
STEPHANIE PETERS

Book design by Karli Kruse
Cover design by Karli Kruse
Cover and title page photographs by Shutterstock Images
Photographs on pages 152–156 by Shutterstock Images

Published in the United States by Jolly Fish Press, an imprint of North Star Editions, Inc.

Library of Congress Cataloging-in-Publication Data (pending)
978-1-63163-909-8 (paperback)
978-1-63163-908-1 (hardcover)

Jolly Fish Press
North Star Editions, Inc.
2297 Waters Drive
Mendota Heights, MN 55120
www.jollyfishpress.com

Printed in the United States of America

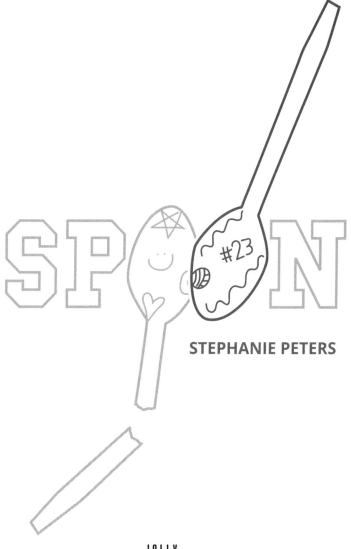

SP⬤N

STEPHANIE PETERS

JOLLY
FiSH
PRESS

Mendota Heights, Minnesota

CHAPTER 1

It's Friday afternoon. Game day for Lynx volleyball. I'm the last to board the bus.

"Macy!" my best friend, Jill, calls. "Over here!"

As I slide in next to her, my ankle twinges with pain. I make a face and lean over to rub it. When I straighten, I see Coach Millburn watching me. I scooch down in my seat.

"Uh, everything all right there, Mace?" Jill asks.

I sigh because everything is *not* all right. I'm about to tell her why when the coach calls for the team's attention.

"This is a big game for us," Coach Millburn says. "The Jaguars won the last two state championships. And they're undefeated so far this season." She smiles. "But who else is undefeated?"

"We are!" we all cry.

"And who is going to stay undefeated today?"

"We are!" we repeat, louder this time.

"And who are we?"

"Linden Lynx! Linden Lynx!"

The bus roars to life. We roar louder—whooping, chanting, and stomping our feet. We quiet down when we pull into the Riverside school parking lot though.

Like all student-athletes, we signed a Code of Conduct at the start of the season. We promised to put our schoolwork before sports. To show good sportsmanship. To be respectful of others. Basically, to be decent human beings.

Showing team spirit doesn't really break the Code. But there could be trouble if anyone complains about us. So, we pipe down.

Most of us do, anyway. When the bus stops, Alliyah jumps up and yells, "Let's kick those Jaguars right in their furry, spotted butts!"

Alliyah is new in town and new to the team this year. She has long, silky black hair, dark eyes, and a warm brown complexion. She's a junior and plays setter, like me. She's got good hands, meaning her passes are clean and accurate. She can serve well too.

And she has a lot of energy. It can be a little much sometimes. Like now.

Liz, one of our captains, thinks so too. "Quiet down, Alliyah," she hisses.

Alliyah looks surprised. When she sees Liz's frown, she rolls her eyes and mumbles, "Sor-*ree*."

Beside me, Jill shakes her head. Not at Liz. At Alliyah.

Jill is not a fan of Alliyah. Hasn't been since the first practice, when Alliyah nailed me in the back of the head with a hard serve and laughed instead of apologizing. Jill has a hot temper. She would have gotten in Alliyah's face that day if I hadn't stopped her.

"It was an accident. So do like the song says, and let it go," I had told her. "Getting angry at the new girl won't be good for the team."

"Fine," Jill huffed. "But she better not mess with you again."

I waved my hand at myself. "Girl, please. No one's gonna mess with this."

She laughed.

But if holding a grudge was an Olympic sport, Jill would win gold. So I'm pretty sure her anger will fire up when she finds out Alliyah is starting today instead of me.

I've owned the starting setter spot all season. But I twisted my ankle during Monday's match. Alliyah took over for me then, and the next two practices too.

Yesterday, though, I convinced Coach Millburn I was fine. And at first, I was. Then my ankle swelled up, and I started limping a little.

After practice, she pulled me aside. "I'm starting Alliyah tomorrow. You'll play, too, but only if your ankle is better."

I stared at the floor and nodded. "It's what's best for the team."

"For tomorrow's match, it is."

I looked up hopefully. "And after that?"

She smiled. "One match at a time."

So, I'm starting on the bench today. But it's not a forever thing.

The bus doors wheeze open. We hustle inside Riverside High.

The Jaguars' gymnasium looks a lot like ours. Light-colored wood floor, basketball hoops, foldout bleachers along both sides. The big difference is the two volleyball championship banners hanging from the rafters.

We're gonna get our first one of those this season, I think.

The Jaguars are warming up. Their shouts mix with the thumps of volleyballs. Music booms from the speakers. Fans pack the stands. Colorful posters decorate the walls. They say things like *THREEPEAT!* and *Bump, Set, Spike, WIN!*

I sit on the visitors' bench. Jill plops down next to me.

"What's that all about?" She jerks her chin at something behind me.

I glance over. Coach Millburn has taken Alliyah aside to talk to her. Alliyah is nodding with excitement. I sigh and tell Jill what's going on.

Her face falls. "You lost your spot because you twisted your ankle. Which was my fault."

"Not true," I protest. "I stepped on your foot."

"Because I went for the ball after you called it!" She points at my ankle. "So, my fault."

"It's fine. And I'm fine."

I lean down and tighten my laces because I can't look her in the eye. But she leans forward too. "Liar," she whispers.

I sigh again. Because she's right.

I love playing volleyball. But I'd do anything to help the Lynx win the championship. Even if that means starting on the sidelines and cheering for my teammates instead of playing.

We do our warm-up drills, then circle up by the visitors' bench. A few of my teammates seem surprised that Alliyah is starting. Most don't though. They must have guessed or known she would replace me today.

Or maybe they hoped she would. After all, I wasn't at my best yesterday. And they want to win as much as I do.

We put our hands together for a team cheer. Alliyah slaps hers on top of the stack.

"Lynx on three," Sandy, our other captain, cries. "One, two, three—"

"LYNX!"

CHAPTER 2

Jill and I sit with our fellow subs. Our starters race onto the court. The Jaguars hit the floor to chants of "THREEPEAT! THREEPEAT!" from their fans. They're going to be tough to beat.

But this afternoon, we're tougher.

To win a match, you must win three out of five games. We win the first two, 25–17 and 25–18. I play in both. But Alliyah is setter most of the time.

Sticking with the winning lineup makes sense. I just wish I was part of that lineup.

We jump to a 22–17 lead in the third game. The Jaguars' coach calls for a time-out.

Liz and Sandy give the other starters a quick pep talk. We listen in from the bench.

"We're close," Liz says. "But we don't have the win yet."

"So stay on your toes," Sandy adds. "Be ready for anything."

Alliyah steps into the middle of the huddle. She makes claws with her hands. "The Lynx are going crush the Jaguars and win this catfight!" She yowls like an angry cat. "Mrrowww!"

Jessie and Emma laugh. Sandy and Kayla grin. Liz just shakes her head.

The time-out ends. Liz, Alliyah, and the others get in ready position to receive the serve—knees bent, arms low and out in front, eyes glued to the girl serving.

The ref's whistle shrieks. The Jaguar tosses the ball in the air. As she slams it over the net, our players spring into action.

Liz sidesteps to get under the ball. Alliyah darts to the right corner by the net. "Here-here-here-here-here!" she yells. Her call is loud and clear, as always.

Liz bumps the ball to her. Alliyah watches it, hands high and close together, fingers wide—the classic set position.

Sandy races forward, ready to leap and blast Alliyah's pass over the net. But at the last second, Alliyah lowers one hand and jumps. She's going for a tip.

Alliyah has tipped the ball over the net several times this match. The move caught the Jaguars off guard and added points to our score.

This time, though, they're ready. "Tip! Tip!" they yell as Alliyah flicks the ball over and down.

"Mine!" Their outside hitter dives across the floor, arm outstretched. She slides her hand, palm down, under the ball. It hits her fingers.

A hard-tipped ball would have bounced up high. But Alliyah's tip was soft. The ball barely clears the girl's knuckles. The point is ours.

Lynx 23, Jaguars 17.

Alliyah starts for the end line to serve.

"Sub!" Coach Millburn suddenly calls. She beckons to Erin and me. "Macy, go in for Alliyah. Erin, you'll sub for Jessie."

My heart leaps as Alliyah and I swap places. Since I

subbed for her, I'm serving. I bounce the ball a few times and take a deep breath.

Two more points, and we defeat the undefeated Jaguars. I want that for us. Badly.

Okay, Macy, I think. *Bring it.*

At the whistle, I toss the ball in the air, take two steps, and jump. Swing my arm around and down. Connect with the ball. Follow it with my eyes as it sails through the air.

And groan when it hits the net.

The hometown fans whoop with glee. Heat rushes to my face. I'm a redhead with pale skin. So my embarrassment shows up like ketchup on a white T-shirt.

Jill catches my eye from the sideline. She pretends to yank a handle downward. That means *flush* in sign language—as in *flush the toilet*. Her deaf cousin taught it to us, along with some other, less appropriate signs. It's her way of telling me to flush my mistake and move on.

I nod. But my gut still clenches. My missed hit gives the Jaguars hope. Hope can be enough for a come-from-behind win. If they beat us, then the loss will be on me.

Then I remember something my sister, Marie, once told me. She's four years older and played volleyball for the Lynx too.

My eighth-grade rec team had just lost a match. At dinner, I complained about a teammate. "It was her fault we didn't win."

Marie pointed her fork at me. "Volleyball is a group sport, Macy. That means no one player gets the credit for a win. And no one player is blamed for a loss."

Thinking about that now helps me get my head back in the game. I flush my mistake and vow to turn the Jaguars' next serve into our point. But their server does it for me by hitting the ball out of bounds.

Lynx 24, Jaguars 18.

We need just one more point to win.

Erin steps to the end line. She serves a floater.

"Short!" the Jaguars yell.

They send the ball back after three touches. Emma passes to me. I set to Sandy. She slams the ball to the far corner.

Their defensive specialist gets under it. Their setter pushes it deep to our backcourt.

Liz is there. Her pass flies toward the sideline. It's going to go out!

I lunge, sticking out my right arm. I connect. The ball launches into the air. It's back in play but flies so high it brushes a championship banner.

When it drops, their setter is waiting. She passes to a hitter. The hitter slams the ball hard. It should be their point.

But Kayla leaps up and blocks it.

The ball hits the floor on the Jaguars' side.

For a split second, the gymnasium is silent.

Then we erupt, yelling and jumping and pumping our fists. We swarm Kayla. Alliyah wraps her in a tight hug. Then she turns and points at me.

"Man, when your arm dig went right to their setter, I thought, *That's it. Their point.*" She grins. "But thanks to Kayla, it all worked out! And I'm sure you'll do better the next time you sub for me."

With that, she elbows her way back into the ring and hugs Kayla again.

I stare after her. *The next time I sub for her?*

CHAPTER 3

Our celebration continues even after we're on the bus. I join in at first. But my heart isn't really in it. I mean, I'm glad we won. But Alliyah's words sting. What if she's right? What if I'm her sub for the next game—and the rest of the season?

I pull out my phone. I have two missed messages. One is from my mom reminding me to text her before I drive home. The other is from Marie. She's in Denmark for a college semester, but she always checks in after a match.

Did you win? Are you gonna be the first Lynx VB championship team?

When Marie was a senior, the Lynx made it to the semi-finals in the playoffs. They needed just two wins to reach the finals. They got the first by beating the Wildcats, the best team in the league that year.

Afterward, she and three seniors went out to celebrate. They ended up at a party. Rumor has it some kids were drinking. Things got out of control. Neighbors called the police.

Marie and her teammates got caught in our car. They weren't arrested, but the Linden High principal found out. She benched the girls for breaking the Code of Conduct.

Four players short, Coach Millburn pulled up girls from junior varsity to fill their spots. Kayla and Liz were two of those players. They were only freshmen. They did their best. But without the seniors, the Lynx were outmatched. They lost badly. Their championship dreams crumbled to dust.

Three years later, coaches and parents still use the "incident" as a warning to players. Marie does too.

"Make better choices than I did, like putting your team and teammates before yourself," she always reminds me.

Jill plops down on the seat beside me. "I heard what Alliyah said to you about you subbing for her." She shakes her head. "Just because she snaked your spot today doesn't mean she gets to keep it."

"She didn't snake my spot," I protest. "Coach gave it to her. And we won the match with her in the starting lineup."

"Yeah, well, we won all our *other* matches when *you* were in the starting lineup," Jill shoots back.

I blink as that sinks in. "Huh. I didn't think of that."

"Yeah, no kidding," she says.

There's a burst of laughter from behind us. Liz made brownies to share, and Alliyah has gone full-on Cookie Monster on one. Crumbs spray from her mouth as she chomps and growls, "Nom-nom-nom-nom-nom!"

Liz joins us with the last brownies. "I'm going to make another batch for team bonding on Monday. It's at your house, right, Jill?"

"Yep. And yum," Jill replies as she takes a bite.

The bus pulls into Linden High. The temperature outside has dropped from chilly to icy. The locker room is plenty warm though. Crowded, too, because the varsity field hockey team is also there. They're quiet because they lost their game in overtime. Out of respect, we take it down a notch.

Alliyah seems oblivious though. She races up to the goalkeeper, who sits slumped on a bench. "Guess what, guess what, guess what?" she gushes. Before the keeper can answer, Alliyah launches into a recap of our match. She describes her tipping plays in detail as I drop my bag on an open bench.

Liz pauses next to me. "What's that keeper's name? Rachel?"

"Rochelle," I correct. "Why?"

"I think she needs rescuing."

Liz talks to Tanya, one of the field hockey team's captains. Tanya glances at Alliyah and Rochelle. "On it." A second later, she's leading her keeper to a quieter spot in the locker room.

"Tanya's a good captain." I nudge Liz. "Like you. And Sandy."

Jill joins us in time to hear that. "We'll be just as good, right, Macy?"

Liz smiles. "You guys want to be co-captains next year?"

Jill points at me. "This one has wanted it since eighth

grade. She'd be awesome, obviously. And I'd be equally awesome as her sidekick."

"Oh, no doubt," Liz says, laughing. "Anyone else want the job?"

As far as I know, none of the other juniors wants to be a captain. Then my gaze lands on Alliyah. She's staring at me as if she's waiting for my answer.

"There might be one or two other juniors who are interested," I reply cautiously.

Jill snorts. "Girl, you know you're a lock for the job."

A week ago, I might have agreed. But I'd been the starting setter in every game then. If Alliyah goes for captain, too, will the other players vote for me—or for the girl who might replace me?

"Hey, you guys want to hang out tomorrow?" Jill asks. "We could binge that new sci-fi show. That actor we love is in it."

I shake my head. "I'm working at the salon all day."

"Gotta grind out my college essay," Liz says.

Jill heaves a sigh. "Guess I'll thirst after Sci-Fi Guy by

myself then." Her phone buzzes. "My mom's here. Either of you need a lift?"

Liz shakes her head, and I pull a key fob out of my sweatshirt pouch.

"I've got wheels." I say it like it's no big deal. It is though. I've only had my driver's license for a month. Today was the first time my folks let me take a car to school.

"Oooo," Jill says, like I'm a big shot.

Laughing, Liz takes off. I cram my backpack full of school supplies and volleyball gear. There's so much stuff the zipper won't close.

Jill grins as I yank everything out. "Good luck with that," she says as she waves goodbye.

The locker room empties as I repack. It's creepy being there alone, so I don't stick around long. The cold hits me in the face when I get outside. Shivering, I text my mom that I'm on my way. Then I reach into my sweatshirt pouch for the car fob.

It's not there. By the time I find it buried in the bottom

of my backpack, it's pitch-black out. Overcast, so no stars. No moon. Just a single streetlamp on the far side of the lot.

I'm not afraid of the dark. But my heart beats fast as I speed-walk to the car.

It beats even faster when something rustles nearby.

Suddenly, a face looms out of the shadows.

I scream.

CHAPTER 4

The face snorts.

"OMG, classic jump-scare!" It's Alliyah. She's laughing.

"I wasn't scared." My racing heart says otherwise. "Just startled."

Alliyah cocks an eyebrow like she doesn't believe me. "Well, anyway, I'm glad you're still here. My mom is stuck in traffic. But now you can drive me home."

She walks to the passenger door like it's a done deal. But it isn't.

"Sorry," I say. "I can't."

"Why not? I only live, like, fifteen minutes that way."

She points in the exact opposite direction from my neighborhood. If I drive her, I won't get home for more than half an hour. I'm tired and hungry. I want a shower. Also, if I'm honest, she's the last person I want to spend more time with today. The comment she made earlier still stings. So does the thought that it might be true. But none of that is why I refuse.

"I only have a junior driver's license," I say. "If I get caught driving anyone but family, I'll lose it for sixty days. And I'll have to pay a big fine to get it back. *If* my parents even let me get it back. They might not because they'll be so pissed at me."

I don't add that if Coach Millburn found out, I'd probably be benched for breaking the Code. I shouldn't need more reasons why driving her is a terrible idea.

But Alliyah just rolls her eyes. "So don't get caught."

She tries the door handle. I don't hit the unlock button.

"I'm sorry," I repeat. "But I can't drive you home."

"Well, what am I supposed to do then? Wait here, by myself, until my mom shows up? Walk the four miles home alone? In the *dark*?"

She glances at the sky and shivers. "I just moved here. I could get lost. Or fall and hurt myself. It's so cold I could get frostbite." Her voice trembles. "Or worse."

I bite my lip. We live in a mountainous area. A lot of our

roads wind through forests. Few of them have sidewalks. Like all kids in Linden, I grew up hearing stories about people losing their way in the dark . . . and being found days or even weeks later.

Team and teammates first, I think, remembering Marie's advice.

I push the unlock button. "I'm still not driving you home. But we can stay warm until your mom gets here."

She narrows her eyes at me. Then she slides onto the passenger seat.

I start the car and crank the heat. The chilly air warms up. But the vibe between us is frosty. After a few minutes, she sighs.

"This is dumb. You're wasting gas. And ruining the environment." She turns to me. "Seriously, I've never seen a single cop on my road. Even if we do pass one, you won't get pulled over if you drive carefully. Plus—"

"Fine." I cut her off because I'm just . . . done. "I'll take you." I flick on the headlights, then fix her with a look. "But if your mom or anyone else asks, I didn't drive you, okay? Linden is a small town. If one person hears about it, everyone will know. Including my parents. Then I'll be in huge trouble."

Alliyah smiles. "It's our secret. Take a left out of the parking lot."

As I turn onto the street, snow starts falling. I've never driven in snow. I grip the steering wheel so tightly my knuckles turn white. Alliyah doesn't seem bothered. She props her feet on the dashboard, connects her phone to the car's Bluetooth, and turns up the volume.

"That was an awesome win today, huh?" she says over the music.

For a second, I wonder if she's going to say something about replacing me at setter. About how she knows it only happened because of my ankle. Or that she felt a little awkward when Coach Millburn told her.

What she says is, "Guess how many points I got with my tips and pushes."

"I didn't keep track," I say through gritted teeth. "And *you* didn't get the points. The *team* did."

She laughs. "Well, sure. But the *team* got the points because of *me*. And the answer is seven. Oh, I love this song!"

She turns up the volume another notch. We come to a crossroad. "Which way?" I yell over a screeching guitar riff.

"What? Oh. That way." She waves her hand. I think she means straight until she yelps, "No! *That* way!" She jabs her thumb to the right.

I turn onto an unfamiliar road. It's snowing harder now.

"Stop! You missed my street!"

Her cry startles me. I slam on the brakes. The car skids on a thin patch of snow, then slows to a stop.

"Jeez, Macy," Alliyah scolds. "Keep us out of the ditch, will you?"

I suck in a shaky breath, back up, and turn onto a narrow, twisting road. Low-hanging tree branches scrape the roof. I strain to see through the whirling snow. My head throbs.

My phone rings. Alliyah's music pauses while Bluetooth announces that my mom is calling.

"Uh-oh." Alliyah covers her mouth with her hands. I can tell she's smiling.

But I'm panicking. I hit the answer button on the steering wheel. "Hey, Mom."

"Are you all right?" Her voice is concerned. "I expected you home twenty minutes ago."

"I, uh, I—" I try to think of a reason I'm so late.

Alliyah stabs a finger at the gas gauge.

"I'm getting gas," I stammer. "There's a line so I'll be a little longer. Sorry, I should have texted."

I hate that I'm lying to my mom. And I feel even worse when she sounds relieved. "No, that's okay. I was just worried because of the snow. Drive safe. Love you."

"Love you too," I mumble.

Alliyah giggles after I hang up. "Man, she's got you leashed, huh?" She has to raise her voice because her music has kicked on again. Even if I felt like answering, she wouldn't hear me.

Finally, we pull into her driveway. She disconnects her phone, but before she gets out, she taps something into the car's GPS system. "Directions from my house to the nearest gas station. You're welcome!"

She disappears into the swirling snow. And I begin the long drive home.

CHAPTER 5

Every Saturday, I work a shift at a beauty salon called Hair We Are. I sweep up clippings, clean out the sinks, do laundry, and restock the shelves. The job isn't glamorous. But the people who work here are cool. They're great with their customers, and they're super nice to me. They even share their tips.

I hope today will be a good tip day because I spent a lot on gas last night.

I arrive at work just before ten o'clock. The stylists look up when the bell over the door jingles.

"Right on time as always, Macy," says Bette, my boss. "You can start by shelving the new products, okay?"

"You got it," I reply.

I tie on my salon apron, put a roll of price stickers and a pen in the pocket, and go to the storeroom. I pass

Cameron on the way. He just finished blow-drying an older woman's hair. She's smiling at herself in the mirror.

This is another reason I like working here. The customers arrive looking like something the cat dragged in. When they leave, they look and feel like a million bucks.

Customers come and go as I sticker and shelve in the front display area. I'm reaching up to put the last bottle in place when someone whispers, "Boo!" right in my ear.

Startled, I drop the bottle. It hits the tile floor and bursts. Shampoo splatters everywhere. I jump back and bump into Alliyah. She's trying not to laugh.

Anger bubbles up inside me. "What are you doing here?"

She holds her hands up in mock surrender. "Whoa, easy, Macy! I'm getting a glow-up—a bunch of hot pink stripes. They'll look super cool in my dark hair." Then she sees my Hair We Are apron. Her eyes go wide. "Hang on. Do you work here?"

People from school sometimes come into the salon when I'm working. Most of them don't treat me any differently. But a few give me the side-eye, like they wouldn't be caught dead doing what I do.

I figure Alliyah would be a side-eye girl. But she surprises me.

"Oh, jeez, Macy, I'm sorry," she says. "I wouldn't have scared you if I knew you worked here. I thought you were buying product." She points at the shattered bottle. "Will you have to pay for that?"

I don't say what I'm thinking: that she should pay for it because she made me drop it. She's a customer. I'm paid to be nice to customers. So, I force a smile. "No biggie. I'll just take it out of my tip money."

"Tip money?" she echoes. "Nice. You must walk out of here with a fat stack, huh?"

I shrug. "Sometimes. Anyway, I better clean up."

Cameron leads Alliyah to his chair. I clean up the mess on the floor. Alliyah stops me on my way back to the sinks.

"Did you know Macy is my teammate?" she tells Cam. "We're really good friends too. Right, Macy?"

"Uh, yeah," I say. But I'm thinking, *We are?*

"Like last night," Alliyah continues. "I was stuck without a ride. She drove me home."

My blood goes cold. Alliyah catches my panicked look in the mirror. Then she gasps.

"Oh, shoot. I wasn't supposed to tell anyone, was I? Because you're not allowed to drive anyone but family yet!" She grabs Cam's arm. "You'll keep her secret, right?"

She gives him a pleading smile. After a second, Cam nods. "Of course I will."

"Phew, that's a relief. I'd hate for Macy to get in trouble."

Bette calls for me to cover the register. I'm still learning how to do that job. So, I make a few mistakes ringing people up. I fix them, but still. I'm feeling flustered when Alliyah comes up to pay.

I get even more flustered when she can't find her debit card.

"I must have left it at home," she says.

"We take cash," I reply.

"This is all I have." She shows me a wrinkled dollar bill with a corner missing.

I sigh and point to a sign with a QR code. "How about a payment app?"

"My mom won't let me get one. And she's at the gym, so it's no use calling her."

"You can't leave without paying," I say, annoyed.

She chews on her lip, thinking. "Maybe you could pay for me."

I raise my eyebrows. "Why would I do that?"

"Because if you don't, you could get in trouble." She lowers her voice and leans in. "You're on the register. If I walk out of here without paying, everyone will know you let me. Then Cam might tell your boss that you drove me last night. Like you said, this is a small town. What if word gets back to your parents? To Coach Millburn, even?" She shakes her head. "Better to pay for me than to risk losing your job. Or getting benched like your sister was."

I flush with anger when she mentions Marie. I want to tell her off. To get Bette and Cam and explain the problem. But they're with clients. The line at the register is growing. Customers are getting impatient. Alliyah has backed me into a corner, and from the smug smile on her face, she knows it.

So even though everything in me is screaming *No!* I pay for her pink stripes. "You're gonna pay me back." I lay her receipt on the counter.

"Oh, sure," she says.

I give her a ten-dollar bill. "That's for Cam's tip. Seal it in one of those little envelopes over there and write his name on the outside. I'll make sure he gets it."

"He deserves every penny. I mean, look at me!" She tosses her pink-streaked hair over her shoulder. It does look great. But seeing her leave looks even better to me.

It's only after she's gone that I realize she didn't take her receipt. I roll my eyes and stuff it in my wallet.

At the end of my shift, I give Cam his tip envelopes. He opens them so he can give me a share.

Inside the one Alliyah left is a single wrinkled dollar bill . . . with the corner missing.

CHAPTER 6

"It was probably a mistake, Macy."

It's Sunday evening, and I'm video chatting with Marie. I just finished telling her everything that happened with Alliyah.

Well, everything except how I drove her home. I'm not sure how she'd take that. Would she be happy that I helped a teammate? Or pissed that I risked losing my license and getting benched?

"That's what Cam thought happened too," I say. "But it still bummed me out."

Marie nods, then yawns. It's after midnight in Denmark. "Just ask Alliyah about it when she pays you back."

I'm not in love with the idea of asking Alliyah if she accidentally switched bills. It would sound like I'm accusing of her stealing. I'm not, but I feel awful that Cam didn't get the tip he deserved. "Yeah, I'll talk to her."

"Of course you will. You do everything your big sister tells you," she says with a smile. "Oh, and Macy?"

"Yeah?"

"Bring it at practice tomorrow, and you'll be back in the starting lineup in no time."

I usually appreciate Marie's support. Tonight, though, it makes me feel pressured. Of course I'll do my best at practice. But will it be enough to start in the next game? If I'm not on the court, how can I ever earn back my spot?

Monday classes drag by as they usually do. After the final bell, I rush to the locker room. Alliyah usually gets to practice first. I hope to catch her alone before anyone else shows up.

I'm in luck. We're the only two there.

"Hey," I say, keeping my voice light. "Those pink stripes look great. Oh, that reminds me . . ." I pull out the salon receipt. "Here's how much they cost."

I don't mention the tip yet.

Or ever, because she throws me a curveball. "Here's

a thought. You don't pester me for money, and I don't tell Coach Millburn or your parents that you drove me home."

My jaw drops. "Are you serious right now?"

"Um, yeah. Seems like a fair trade to me. Oh, and I have technology on my side. Your car's GPS will show you went from my house to a gas station."

I go still because she's right. The navigation system logs recent routes. If Mom or Dad check it, they'll know I lied about coming right home.

I feel like I've been caught in a trap with no way to escape. I could lash out like a caged lion, but what good would that do? Scowling, I put the receipt back in my pocket and move to my locker.

Our teammates start filtering in then. Liz looks from Alliyah to me curiously. I force myself to smile, then change into my volleyball clothes.

I'd planned to follow Marie's advice and give it my all at practice today. To show the coach that I belong in the starting lineup. To remind my teammates that I could help us win. But after my run-in with Alliyah, I feel deflated, like a balloon with a slow leak. It doesn't help that Coach Millburn puts Alliyah with the starters for a scrimmage.

Alliyah serves first. She sends the ball to the back left corner. Jill bumps it to me. I set to Heather, our backup middle blocker. As she hits the ball, Alliyah and Kayla leap up with a double block. The ball strikes Alliyah's forearms and bounces back to us. I forget to cover the open space behind Heather. The ball hits the floor.

The starters whoop. I shake my head. "Sorry," I mutter.

They get a few more points. Then Erin clocks a nice cross-court hit that Liz can't get to in time. Our point, and now my serve.

I head to the end line with the ball. I bounce it a few times. Then I toss it high and step into my jump.

At that same moment, Alliyah cries out, "Ball's up!"

Tweet!

Play stops at Coach Millburn's whistle. Yelling during an opponent's serve isn't against the rules. But she considers it unsportsmanlike behavior. She warned us at the start of the season not to do it.

All eyes turn to Alliyah. She smacks her forehead. "My bad! Sorry, Coach! Sorry, Macy! We used to yell stuff like that on my old team. It won't happen again."

"See that it doesn't," Coach Millburn says sternly. "Macy, serve it up."

Maybe it's wrong, but hearing Alliyah get chewed out gives me a little boost. When I serve, the ball rockets over the net, low and fast. It's going right where I aimed it—just inside their right sideline.

"Mine!" Liz charges forward. But she stumbles as her forearms connect with the ball. The pass launches toward the bleachers instead of Alliyah's hands.

It should be our point. But Alliyah doesn't give up. "I got it!" Eyes glued to the ball, she bolts for the stands—and right into the ball cart! It topples over, taking her with it.

"Oh my God!" Liz races to Alliyah's side.

Coach Millburn gets there first. She kneels, her face lined with concern. "Are you hurt?"

"I'm okay." Alliyah gives a shaky laugh as she gets to her feet. "Guess I should have let that one go."

"Phew!" Sandy says. "I thought we lost our star setter!"

Several players nod their agreement. Alliyah laughs. "It'll take more than a wrestling match with a ball cart to sideline me!"

Coach Millburn claps her hands. "Okay, everybody, get back on the court. Macy, you're still serving."

I nod. But the deflated balloon feeling is back. *Star setter,* I think. *That's Alliyah. Not me.*

That thought haunts me through the rest of practice. In the locker room afterward, my teammates surround Alliyah, who jokes about her fall.

"Sorry again for that bad pass," Liz apologizes. "I'm a little out of it. I was up all night working on my college essay."

"All night?" Alliyah laughs. "Are you writing a novel or something?"

Liz turns red. "No, I have a learning disability. So writing can be hard for me."

"Oh. Did not know that about you," Alliyah says. "Hey, I'm sure your essay will be great."

Her tone is kind. But when she turns away from Liz, I see her smirk, like Liz's challenges are a big joke to her.

Everything in me screams to come to Liz's defense. But I'm worried Liz will be embarrassed if I do. And that my teammates will think I'm starting problems because I'm upset Alliyah replaced me. I don't want to rock the boat, not when we're so close to our goal of making the playoffs.

And yeah . . . I'm worried that Alliyah might get back at me by telling them and Coach Millburn about the car ride.

So, I swallow my frustration. It burns the whole way down.

CHAPTER 7

After practice, Liz gives Jill and me a ride to Jill's house for team bonding. It's something we do the day before most matches. Usually, it's a lot of fun.

I'm not into it today though. But I don't want to kill the vibe for my friends. So, I pretend everything is fine.

"I heard you and Sandy went to a captains' meeting last week," I say to Liz. "What was that all about?"

She shrugs. "It was a leadership thing, basically. Who to talk to if a player's grades are dropping. How to boost team morale if you're having a losing season. What to say to a player who has a bad game."

"Did it cover how to deal with a teammate who steals another teammate's starting position?" Jill pipes up from the back seat. "Because I have questions."

I'd use the sign for *not cool* if I knew it. Instead, I sign *bad*, pressing the fingers of my right hand against my lips, and then pushing them away and down.

Liz catches the gesture and smiles. "One of these days, you guys will have to teach me some signs. But to answer your question, we didn't cover that."

"Bummer. I guess we're on our own with Alliyah," Jill says.

"Is that who you're talking about?" Liz jokes. "I had no idea!"

We pull into Jill's driveway. Liz grabs the brownies she brought. Inside, we help carry bags of snacks and bowls of fruit to the dining room. It'll be a tight squeeze with the regular table, a foldout table, and twelve chairs. But we're used to squishing in together at these things.

The other girls arrive. Emma glances around. "What, no games?"

"Oh, I got game." Jill grabs two decks of cards and a pack of white plastic spoons. "Get your snack on, everyone. Then we'll play Spoons. Ice cream comes later."

We eat like we're bears just out of hibernation, then clear off the tables. Jill counts out eleven spoons and sets them in a wide ring in the middle. She deals each of us four cards.

"The object is to get four of a kind," she says. "The dealer draws a card from the deck. If she can use it, she keeps it and discards a card from her hand. If she can't use it, she discards it and draws the next card."

"And the next person picks up the discarded card, and the whole thing keeps going from person to person, right?" Sandy chimes in.

Jill nods. "When someone gets four of a kind, they grab a spoon. Then everyone else grabs one too."

"But there are only eleven spoons and twelve of us," Heather points out.

"Ooo, look who can count!" Alliyah says with a laugh. Others laugh too. Heather frowns.

"If you don't get a spoon," Jill says, "you get an S. First person who spells out *spoon* loses."

Alliyah scoops up the deck. "I call dealer!"

She draws a card immediately. As the rest of us scramble to pick up our hands, she discards it. Nell picks it up, mutters "Nope," and puts it down.

The only sounds in the room are murmurs and the whisper of cards being discarded. There's an undercurrent of excitement though. Who will get four of a kind first? Who won't get a spoon?

I'm reaching for a card when I see a flash of movement. Kayla has snatched a spoon! Mayhem breaks out as the rest of us grab one. Nell and Alliyah go for the same spoon. Nell comes up empty-handed.

"Yaaassss!" Alliyah waves the spoon overhead. "Suck it, Nell!"

"Hey, you scratched me," Nell says. A thin line of red appears on the back of her hand.

"Well, I am a Lynx." Alliyah curls her hands into claws and growls.

Nell smiles uncertainly, then gets up to clean and bandage the scratch.

We play more rounds when she returns. Liz loses

three times in a row. She loses a fourth time too. But only because Sandy yanks the spoon out of her grasp.

"That was mine!" Liz fumes.

"Really?" Sandy examines the spoon. "I don't see your name on it."

Liz lunges to grab it. Sandy twists away and holds the spoon behind her. "You want it? Come get it!"

Then Jill snatches the spoon away. She nests it with the one she'd grabbed. "If you two can't play nice, neither of you gets a spoon," she scolds.

"Or maybe I get both of those spoons, *plus* mine." With lightning-quick speed, Kayla plucks the spoons away from Jill. She stands up and raises them high in triumph. "Yaaasss! Winner, winner, chicken dinner!"

Erin, Nell, and I leap to our feet and try to reach the spoons. Kayla just laughs. "Dang, you guys are short. I'm not even on my tippy-toes." She doesn't see Liz stand up on the chair behind her.

"Thank you very much," Liz says, taking the spoons.

Kayla looks so outraged, I burst out laughing.

"Yo, yo, yo!" Alliyah suddenly cries. "I just got a great idea for a new game!" She turns to Jill. "But first, how about that ice cream?"

CHAPTER 8

Jill and I hand out bowls of ice cream and clean plastic spoons.

"So, what is this game?" Heather asks Alliyah through a mouthful of chocolate chip ice cream.

"I call it . . ." Alliyah pauses for dramatic effect. "Spoon!"

"Uh, isn't that the game we were just playing?" Emma says.

"No, that was Spoons, plural," Alliyah corrects. "In that game, you can only grab a spoon if you or someone else gets four of a kind." Her eyes gleam. "In Spoon, you can grab one anytime."

Nell wrinkles her nose. "We just toss spoons on the table and then yell 'Go!' or something?"

"No." Alliyah licks ice cream from her spoon, then holds it up. "We take our spoons home. We decorate them. Then we bring them with us everywhere we go. All day, all night, they're with us. And we protect them."

"Protect them from what?" Jessie asks.

"From each other. See, the object of Spoon is to steal each other's spoons. If you lose yours, you're out of the game. The last person with a spoon wins." She looks around the table. "So, you guys want to play?"

Sandy gives a thumbs-up. "Sounds like fun. I'm in."

"Me too," Lynn says.

"Hang on a sec," I say. All eyes turn to me. "Grabbing a spoon from someone could be a little dangerous." I point to Nell's scratched hand.

"And we can't practice or play while holding spoons," Liz adds.

"We could leave our spoons in our lockers during volleyball," Sandy suggests.

"And the grabbing thing?" Nell asks.

Alliyah thinks for a moment. Then she says, "Okay, no grabbing or stealing. To get someone's spoon, you must first show yours. Then the other person has five seconds to show hers. If she does, you both keep your spoons. Like this."

She whirls toward Jessie. "Spoon! Five! Four! Thr—"

"Ah!" Jessie snatches her spoon out of her bowl. Drops of melted ice cream land in her hair. "Spoon! Spoon!" she yelps.

We all crack up.

"What would happen if I didn't show my spoon in time?" Jessie asks as she wipes the ice cream away.

"This." Alliyah reaches over and snaps Jessie's spoon in half.

Jessie pouts. "Aw, I wasn't done with my ice cream!"

Jill slides her a fresh spoon.

"Any other questions?" Alliyah asks.

I wave my hand. "How about we include the junior varsity players? Make Spoon an all-volleyball thing?"

Liz nods. "Great idea, Macy."

Alliyah clears her throat. "Does that include the coaches too?"

Liz and Sandy exchange glances. As captains, they usually tell Coach Millburn about team activities. After a moment, Sandy shrugs. "I'm good with keeping this just among us. What do you think, Liz?"

Liz gives a quick nod. "Sure. As long as it doesn't get out of control."

"It won't," Alliyah promises. She raises her spoon like a sword. "To Spoon!"

"To Spoon!" we echo.

The team hangout breaks up then. Liz and I help Jill clean up, then Liz gives me a lift home.

"You sure you're okay with this whole Spoon thing?" I ask on the ride.

Liz shrugs. "Yeah, since it's a team bonding thing. We captains are always looking to do stuff like that." She smiles. "You'll find that out next year, I bet."

Her smile fades as she pulls into my driveway. She puts the car in park and turns to me. "Macy, listen, about Alliyah starting instead of you . . . if you need to talk, I'm here to listen."

Her kindness almost makes me spill the tea about Alliyah. But I just nod and say, "Thanks. It doesn't feel great to be sidelined. I'm trying to stay positive though."

"Good. Positive is the right attitude for a player." She glances at me. "And for a captain."

"You always come off as positive," I assure her.

She laughs. "I'm talking about you."

I'm grateful for her support. But I can't help but blurt, "But if Alliyah ends the season as a starter, I bet she'll get more votes."

That thought has crossed my mind a few times in the past week. I haven't said it out loud before though.

"I wasn't a starter last year," Liz points out. "So, you have as much of a chance as any other junior. More, if you ask me. Because I'll be talking you up!"

I grin. "That's why you're my favorite captain. Seriously, though . . . thanks." I get out of the car and wave goodbye with my white plastic spoon.

After I shower, I turn that spoon into a mini Macy, complete with red yarn hair and a green felt volleyball jersey. I'm gluing on googly eyes and getting excited about the game when my phone buzzes.

It's a text from Jill: **Have you seen this???** It's followed by a social media post from Alliyah. I click it.

Epic Game Invite! a banner reads. Then Alliyah appears on-screen. She's holding her spoon and grinning. "Hey, Linden High! You want in on the hottest game around? Then scroll down and get your Spoon on!"

"What the *what*?" I mutter.

I scroll to the bottom and click the *Join* link. A list of Spoon rules pops up. I don't bother to read them. Instead, I switch back to Jill's text.

She invited the whole school? Unbelievable. Are you still going to play?

Well, I'm not gonna watch from the sidelines, Jill replies. **And neither are you! Right?**

I reply with a picture of my spoon. **Can't let this bad girl go to waste.**

Our exchange is interrupted by a text from Alliyah to our volleyball group chat.

Hey guys! it says. **If you haven't seen it, I've got the whole school in on Spoon!**

I saw, Liz responds. **How did that happen?**

My BFF Rochelle! Alliyah texts. **She blabbed about it to the other field hockey players. They asked to join, and it exploded from there. It's going to be awesome!**

She ends with a series of excited-face emojis.

Jill shoots me an emoji of the green vomit-face in our private text thread. I send back the eye roll one. Then I put my phone on silent and pick up my spoon. What is the game going to be like now that everyone at school can play?

CHAPTER 9

I'm walking across the school parking lot the next morning when Daniel and Marco, two senior soccer players, run toward me.

"Spoon!" Marco yells.

"Yeah, spoon," Daniel echoes.

Marco's spoon looks like a three-year-old decorated it. But Daniel made his into a little alien with wide black eyes and green skin. I don't admire it, though, because they've begun the countdown.

"Five!" they shout. "Four!"

I pull Mini Macy from my back pocket. "Nice try."

"You escaped this time because you saw us coming," Marco says. "Next time though? Total sneak attack."

"I'll be watching." I point two fingers at my eyes, then at them.

They laugh. Marco heads off to find another target. Daniel walks with me into school.

"You guys have a home match today, right?" he says.

"Yep. Is there a soccer game too?"

"Not until tomorrow."

We reach my locker. I figure he's going to take off. Instead, he leans against the wall and faces me. "Maybe I'll come see you play after our practice."

My insides give a little happy dance. I got to know Daniel this summer when we both worked part-time at a sports camp for kids. He's tall with dark skin and close-cropped black hair. He plays basketball and tennis as well as soccer. He's not arrogant about it though. In fact, he's flat-out nice. And he has a killer smile.

A freshman girl interrupts us. "Spoon!" she shrieks. She waves a glitter-covered spoon like a magic wand.

Daniel and I whip out our spoons. The girl leaves, disappointed. Daniel leaves too. But he sends me a smile before he goes. "See you later, Macy."

"Yeah, see you." I hope I do.

I meet up with Jill at our usual spot by the water fountain. Then we dive into the sea of students.

People usually chat and laugh in the hallway. But this morning, I mostly hear shouts of "Spoon!" followed by countdowns.

Jill and I fend off a few attacks. And I knock a skinny sophomore with glasses out of the game. I feel triumphant when I snap his spoon. Then I feel terrible because he's so bummed out.

"Sorry," I mumble. I hand him back the pieces. He throws the broken spoon in the trash and storms off.

Jill shakes her head. "Well, this is turning into a fun game."

"Yeah. From now on, I'll stick to showing my spoon instead of breaking others'."

"Good idea," she says.

We part ways. As I enter my English classroom, I feel a gentle tug on my back pocket. Someone is trying to steal my spoon!

"Hey!" I whirl around.

Marco freezes. Then he drops his hand and smiles sheepishly. "Um . . . spoon?"

I wave a finger under his nose. "Don't even think about counting down," I warn. "And for the record, stealing spoons isn't allowed."

"Actually, it is." He pulls up the Spoon rules on his phone. Number four: *If you can steal a spoon, go for it!*

I frown. "Seriously? Last night, we agreed on no stealing." I want to text Alliyah about it. But then I see our teacher approaching.

"Heads up," I say to Marco.

We're not allowed to use phones in classrooms. If he's caught with his, he'll get detention. Detention means he'll miss practice. Missing practice means he'll have to sit out his next soccer game. Marco quickly stows his phone as we take our seats.

"Thanks. I'm still coming for your spoon though," he murmurs.

I zip my spoon in my hoodie pocket. "And I'll be ready."

I'm on high alert for the rest of the day. Just hearing

someone yell, "Spoon!" makes me jump. And keeping my spoon zipped in my hoodie wasn't my best idea. More than once, I nearly run out the five-second countdown before I get it free.

I survive the day. But I sigh with relief when I stow Mini Macy in my gym locker.

Rochelle is walking past when I do. She laughs. "I thought having field hockey balls hurled at me was stressful. But this?" She looks at her spoon and shakes her head. "This is next level."

"You could always get timed out," I say. "You know, *accidentally*."

Rochelle snorts. "I would, except Al would make fun of me."

"Al?"

"Sorry, I mean Alliyah. We grew up in the same neighborhood before I moved to Linden. Her nickname was Al back then."

"Did you guys stay in touch?" I ask, curious.

"Nah, we were too young for phones, and my parents

didn't really hang out with her mom. We had no way to get together." She hesitates, then adds, "I was okay with that actually."

"Really? Why?"

"She's intense. If we played a game, she had to win. If she didn't, she threw a fit. I'm talking full-on tantrum." She looks at her spoon again, then tosses it in her locker with a smile. "She's mellowed out since then though. Now she just likes to have fun."

I'm not so sure that's true.

The Easterly Lions arrive as we hit the court. Alliyah chuckles when she sees their yellow-and-black uniforms. "They look like bumblebees!"

Sandy frowns. "Dude, be quiet, will you?"

I'm surprised it's Sandy scolding her until Liz whispers, "Alliyah broke Sandy's spoon outside the locker room."

Junior varsity plays first. My teammates and I sit together in the stands. Some do their homework or put in their earbuds. But I cheer on the younger girls. It felt good when the varsity players rooted for me when I was on JV. Plus, the only other fans are their parents.

I pay attention for another reason too. If we make playoffs, the top JV players will be added to the varsity roster. They'll practice with us. That way, they'll be ready to sub in if something happens to one of us . . . or if one of us gets benched. Not that any of us are planning to get benched.

Then again, Marie and her teammates didn't either.

JV matches are best of three. Our girls win in record time, two games to none. My teammates and I hurry to the court to high-five our congrats. I call each of the girls by name—something else I remember liking when I played JV. Liz smiles at me when she hears me.

So does Daniel. I didn't see him come into the gym. But now he's with the other home-team spectators. I smile back as I hit the court for warm-ups. Then I remember I'm not starting today. And my smile slips away.

CHAPTER 10

At the start of our season, our fans were mostly parents and JV players. But as our wins kept coming, our fan base grew.

Today, the home spectator area is crammed full of students. And every single one of them is playing Spoon. At least, that's what it sounds like as we warm up.

"Spoon!" some yell while others call out, "Five! Four! Three! Two! One!"

But those shouts are nothing compared to when Alliyah steps to the end line for her first serve.

"Go get 'em, Spoon!" someone cries.

The student fans immediately start chanting, "Spoon! Spoon! Spoon!"

I glance at Alliyah, worried the chant will throw her off her game. But she's grinning from ear to ear.

The fans quiet down when the ref signals Alliyah to

serve. She tosses the ball high, leaps, and swings her arm. *Whump!* It's a line drive so powerful the Lions' back row moves away from the ball, not toward it.

"Spoooooooooon!" one fan shouts. Others join in.

Alliyah bursts out laughing, then serves to the deep right corner. This time, the Lions' defensive specialist does her job. *Thud!* The ball arcs off her forearms toward their setter. She looks like she's going to set her outside hitter. Instead, she pushes it behind her to her right-side hitter.

Jessie is alone on that side of the net. When the Lions' hitter connects, she jumps with her arms high over her head. The ball goes over her fingertips. It's going to be the Lions' point.

Except it isn't. Alliyah is right behind Jessie. She bumps the ball to Kayla, who slams it over the net for our third point.

A girl in the stands starts a new chant. "S! P! O-O-N!" she calls out. She adds claps in time with the letters. Everyone around her picks up the rhythm.

"Uh-oh," Jill murmurs. She jerks her chin toward the

Lions' bench. Their subs are all glaring at our student section. Their coach is too.

"Can we get in trouble if our fans are out of control?" Jill whispers.

"I don't think so," I say. But their unsportsmanlike behavior doesn't make us look good, especially when our starting setter is clearly into it. I'm almost relieved when we lose the next point. At least it shuts down our fans.

The peace lasts as long as the Lions have the serve. Which isn't very long. The yells grow louder as we rack up points. I get into the game midway through. But by then, it's a done deal. We win 25–16.

As we switch sides for the next game, I hear Daniel talking to Marco. "Dude, chill out with the Spoon stuff, will you?"

Marco rolls his eyes. "You're just pissed because I knocked you out of the game."

"I don't care about that," Daniel says. "The chanting is just annoying. And it could come back to bite the volleyball team."

Marco sees that I'm listening and smirks. "Why do you care? You trying to white knight one of the players or something?"

I look away, blushing. I don't need Daniel to save me or the team. But I don't hate that he might want to.

I'm so caught up in that thought that I miss it when Coach Millburn calls my name. Luckily, Liz hears. She pulls me into the huddle.

"Macy, you'll start this game," Coach Millburn says.

"What? Why?" Alliyah blurts out. "We're winning with me at setter."

"True," Coach Millburn says. "And we'll win with Macy out there too."

For a split second, I think Alliyah is going to keep arguing. But the stern look on Coach's face stops her. "Of course we will." She smiles at me before turning back to the coach. "I just hope the fans are okay with the change."

Coach Millburn narrows her eyes. "The fans are *why* I'm making the change. We'll talk about that after the match. Starters, onto the court."

As I hurry to my position, I glance back at Jill. She tilts her head toward Alliyah. Then she widens her eyes and flares her fingers away from her hair—the universal sign for "mind blown."

I make a fist and knock at the air, sign language for "yes." Though I'm not sure what blew my mind more: Alliyah questioning the roster change or Coach Millburn's response to the fans.

It doesn't matter, I decide. I mentally make the flush sign to clear my head. It's game time, and I need to help the team win.

Unlike the noisy first game, the second one starts out much quieter. There's the thump of the ball, of course, and the squeak of sneakers on the polished wooden floor. And my teammates and I yell "Here!" and "Mine!" and shout one another's names. The fans clap when we get points. But no one chants or shouts "Spoon!" or counts down from five.

I should be happy about that. Instead, I'm a little embarrassed. I knew the "Spoon!" cheers were for Alliyah and that I'm playing now because Coach didn't like them.

Still, it feels like a slap in the face to not hear them when I'm on the court.

We're winning though. So, I focus on each point. On being in the right place to get a pass. On sending the ball where it needs to go. On serving with power and accuracy. I celebrate good plays with my teammates and help them shake off bad moments.

And I pretend it doesn't bother me when the student fans whoop for Alliyah when she subs for me.

We win the second game, 25–13. Alliyah starts the third. The crowd stomps, claps, and cheers. The sounds fire Alliyah up. I played well. But she's playing like a pro. Back sets, pushes, tips, serves, digs, pancakes—she's doing it all, and the fans love it.

We win the third game 25–11 to keep our undefeated record. I'm glad, of course, though I feel bad for the Lions. They don't say a word as they file out of the gym. But a few of them shoot us dirty looks.

"Yikes."

I turn to see Liz walking toward me. I think she's talking

about the Lions until she nods toward the bleachers. Our student section is littered with broken plastic spoons. The custodian is staring at the mess and shaking his head.

"Should we help clean up?" I whisper.

"No time. Coach has called a team meeting." She lets out a long breath as she starts for the locker room. "And I don't think it's to congratulate us."

CHAPTER 11

The locker room is empty except for our team. The field hockey and girls' soccer teams have away games. The place feels bigger without them. Not as much fun either.

Coach Millburn paces back and forth in front of the team. She runs her hand through her short brown hair. When she finally stops and turns to us, her face is grim.

"I just had a very uncomfortable conversation with the Lions' coach," she says. "He tore into me because of our fans. Your classmates. He said their behavior was the worst he's ever experienced at a sports event. That it ruined the match for him and his players."

She pauses, her lips pressed tight together. "Quite frankly, it ruined the match for me too. I'm especially disappointed in the student-athletes in the crowd. They all signed the same Code of Conduct you did. But today, they chose to ignore it. And in doing so, they embarrassed themselves, our team, and our school."

Even though I wasn't one of the fans, shame floods my veins. I wish the floor would open up and swallow me whole. My teammates feel the same way. Some hang their heads. Others shift in their seats. Liz pulls her knees in tight to her chest.

Coach Millburn clears her throat. "Now, can someone please explain why everyone was chanting *spoon*?"

Heads lift. All eyes turn to look at Alliyah. I wait for her to say something. To at least apologize for inviting the whole school to play.

When she says nothing, I wrestle with whether to tell the coach about Spoon myself. It seems like the right thing to do. But will Alliyah get in trouble? My teammates wouldn't thank me if that happened. So, I stay quiet like everyone else.

Everyone except Liz.

"Spoon is a game we came up with at our last team hangout," she says. She briefly describes the rules. "It was supposed to be a fun team bonding activity. But word got out, and now the whole school is playing."

"I see." Coach Millburn's gaze flicks to Alliyah, then back to Liz. She sighs. "I wish I could order you to stop playing. But that's not my job. Instead, I ask you to be careful. To remember that you signed the Code. So, if you play Spoon, stay in control of yourselves. Or better yet, walk away from it."

She runs her hand through her hair again. "There's one other thing I'd like you to do."

"Just name it, Coach, and we'll do it!" Sandy says.

Coach Millburn gives a small smile. "I'd like you to reach out to your fans. Ask them to be respectful at our matches. And to leave their spoons behind."

Nell raises her hand. The thin scratch is a line of red on her skin. "What if they don't listen?"

"They might not," Coach admits. "But if you don't ask, they'll keep doing the same thing. Principal Radcliffe and other administrators might get involved. Things did not go well for us the last time that happened."

I know she's thinking about Marie and the other seniors who were benched because I am too. I need her to know that I agree with everything she's saying. "We'll talk to them," I tell her.

I'm about to add that we'll talk about ending Spoon, too, when Coach Millburn's phone rings.

"All right. You're free to go. Congrats on the win and on keeping your undefeated record." She pumps a fist as she hurries to her office. "Go, Lynx!"

"Lynx!" we echo. Then players scatter.

"That was rough," Jill murmurs as we head to our lockers.

"Yeah, but necessary."

"For sure." She starts shoving her things into her backpack. "I'm going to corner that knucklehead Marco. Read him the riot act. Or maybe the Code."

I hide a smile. Jill and Marco dated off and on during the summer. Knucklehead or not, she's still into him.

"I'll say something to Daniel," I tell her.

Now it's her turn to smile. But she doesn't hide it.

"Shut up." I spin my lock but mess up the combination twice.

Jill laughs. "Uh-oh! Did thinking about Daniel make you forget your combo?"

"I hope not, since it's my birthday." I rattle off the month, day, and year.

She rolls her eyes. "Girl, we've been friends forever. I know your birthday is June 25. That date has been stuck in my brain since first grade. Ever since you cried because my family went on vacation and I couldn't come to your party."

I put my hand on my heart. "That still hurts right here."

"We sent you a present."

I nod. "Swim fins and a snorkel."

"Yes. It was a great gift. What's not great? Using your birthday as your combo. Do you also use *password* as your password?"

I pretend to be shocked. "What? I'm not supposed to do that?"

She sighs dramatically. "Just change your combo before someone breaks into your locker."

I salute, then spin the dial again. This time, the lock clicks open. I take out my hoodie. As I do, Alliyah pops out from behind the lockers.

"Spoon!" she hisses gleefully.

She sticks her spoon in my face. The pink and black ribbons she used for hair tickle my nose. I pull back and fumble to unzip my hoodie pocket.

"Five!"

Then I pause. *I could let time run out. It's what Coach would want me to do.*

"Four!"

Images suddenly flash across my brain. Alliyah saying nothing while Liz explained Spoon.

My ten-dollar bill in her hand. Her one-dollar bill in Cam's tip envelope.

"Three!"

Her feet propped on the dashboard of my dad's car.

"Two!"

Alliyah heading onto the court . . . and me sitting on the bench.

"On—"

I yank out my spoon.

Alliyah grins. "Glad you're still in the game." She leans forward and adds in a whisper, "But you won't be for long."

CHAPTER 12

I don't plan to talk to Daniel until tomorrow. But to my surprise, he's hanging around outside the gym when Jill and I leave.

"Hey, Macy," he calls. "Got a sec?"

"Go get it, girl." Jill shoots me with finger guns as she backs away. I return fire with daggers from my eyes. Then I hurry to meet Daniel.

"Hey. What's up?"

"Just wanted to make sure you and your teammates are okay." He shifts his backpack to his other shoulder. "I saw Coach Millburn getting chewed out by the Easterly coach."

"Yeah." I tell him about our team meeting and the broken spoons in the stands. "Can you say something to the other soccer players? Ask them to talk to their friends too?"

"Absolutely."

He pulls out his phone. His thumbs dance over the screen. I hear a *whoosh* as he sends a text. A moment later, my phone pings.

"That's from me," he says. "I got your number from Liz. Hope you don't mind."

"I don't." I open the text—and pray my blush doesn't show up in the screen's light.

Hey, guys, it reads. **Spoon got a little too crazy at the volleyball game today. We don't want the girls to get in trouble, right? So come cheer them on—but leave Spoon out of it.**

I look up to see Daniel watching me.

"Does it sound okay? I'll send it to our group chat right now if it does," he says.

"It sounds great. Thanks."

"No problem." He hits a few buttons. There's another *whoosh* as we walk across the parking lot to his car. "You need a lift home?"

I wish that I did. "No, I've got my dad's car today."

"Another time, maybe." He reaches for the door handle,

then pauses. Chews his bottom lip. "Or maybe I could pick you up at your house sometime? We could go see a movie or grab food or something."

My heart soars. "We could do that."

He grins broadly. "Awesome. I'll text you."

I grin back. "You better."

The next few days are a blur of classes, practices, and Spoon. Mini Macy's yarn hair and googly eyes are looking pretty rough by Friday.

Also looking rough? Me. Because Spoon is stressing me out. So is the upcoming match against the Sylvan Coyotes. We squeaked out a win against them earlier in the season. They're going to want to crush us in front of their fans today.

Thinking about fans makes me anxious too. We spread the word to behave, just like I told Coach Millburn we would. Daniel said his teammates promised to behave. And since it's an away game, our fan base should be small anyway.

But until the first serve, there's no way of knowing what will happen.

The locker room is crowded after school. The field hockey and girls' soccer teams are also traveling to Sylvan. Like us, they're all putting their spoons in their lockers. Alliyah notices too. She doesn't look happy about it. But she keeps quiet for once.

I wore a cute dress today instead of my usual leggings and hoodie. Jill smirked when she first saw me. I said it wasn't because of Daniel. But we both knew I was lying.

At my locker, I kick off my ankle boots and switch my dress and black tights for my volleyball shorts and team jersey. Jill pulls out her uniform and a red sports drink. She changes quickly, then takes a long gulp of her drink. That's when Alliyah pounces.

"Spoon!"

Sputtering, Jill stumbles backward. She trips over my boots. The red drink spills all down her jersey.

Alliyah is laughing so hard she can't even start her countdown.

"Don't bother," Jill says. "I'm out." She digs out her spoon and snaps it in half. Then she peels off her jersey and stalks to the restroom.

I hurry after her. "Hey, you okay?"

"No. I'm sticky. And I'm sick of Alliyah." She pumps runny orange soap onto her jersey and starts scrubbing. "I should have kept playing Spoon just to beat her."

I laugh. "It would have killed her to lose to you."

"Yeah." Jill stops scrubbing and looks at me. "But imagine if she loses to you. Oh, man, that'd be so awesome! Tell me you'll take her down, Macy."

I bite my lip. Playing Spoon has been stressful. But I'm tired of Alliyah getting away with whatever she wants. Will it hurt the team if I beat her at Spoon? I don't think so. It might even help, because I doubt the game will continue if she's knocked out.

"Okay, I'll keep playing," I say.

Jill grins, then smacks the hand dryer button. She turns her head to one side when the hot air blows on her shirt.

"God, the smell of this soap makes me feel sick. I'm getting a headache just being in the same room with it."

The machine shuts off. She pulls the shirt over her head. Her face twists in disgust. "Ugh, gross. It's like putting on a wet bathing suit." She lifts a sleeve to her nose. "Seriously, I'm going to gag."

She says it jokingly, but she does look a little green. I push her arm away from her nose, then draw back. She wasn't kidding—her jersey does smell bad. "Let's go outside. The fresh air will help."

Liz comes into the restroom as we're going out. She does a double take when she sees Jill. "You look awful. Like, go see the school nurse awful. Do you need to go home? I can let Coach know if you do."

"It's just a headache," Jill says. Then she looks more closely at Liz. "You don't look so good yourself, you know."

She's right. Our captain has dark circles under her eyes. Her skin is paler than usual. Her freckles stand out like pepper on mashed potatoes.

Liz sighs. "Yeah, another long night working on college stuff. Anyway, it's time to get on the bus, guys. So grab your gear. And Jill?"

"Yeah?"

"Sit far away from me. Your shirt reeks like that nasty school soap."

CHAPTER 13

The Sylvan High gymnasium is brand-new. Outside its double doors is a concession stand that sells bowls of chili, hot dogs, and big pretzels. Inside, a running track circles the second level, and windows let in the late afternoon light. Or they would if the sky wasn't so cloudy.

"Whoa," I say, gazing around. "Fancy."

We drop our gear at the varsity visitors' bench and gather around Coach Millburn.

"Same starting lineup as the last two matches," she informs us. She nods toward the stands. "But not the same fan base, I see."

I glance over my shoulder. Only a small cluster of people are in the visitors' section. None of them are Linden High students.

We fan out onto the court to warm up. Midway through

drills, the skies outside open up. Heavy rain hammers the windows and roof.

Nell shakes her head. "Man, I'm glad I don't play an outdoor sport."

"Same," I say with a laugh.

I don't give the rain another thought until I'm on the bench. That's when a bright flash lights up the windows.

Beside me, Kayla startles. "Was that lightning?" She peers up at the windows, eyes wide. Her voice is fearful.

A low rumble of thunder follows the lightning.

Her eyes go even wider. She hugs herself tightly. "Oh, man. I *hate* thunderstorms."

"Really? Why?" I ask.

"A few years ago, a lightning bolt hit a tree outside my window. A huge branch crashed into my room. It landed on my bed." She shudders. "I'd just gotten up. If I hadn't, that branch would have crushed me."

Liz is sitting on Kayla's other side. She puts her arm around her. "You know you're safe in here, right?"

Kayla nods. But she keeps staring at the windows. When another flash of lightning turns them white again, she hugs herself even tighter.

"Hey, check it out." Nell is coming back from filling up her water bottle. She jerks her chin at the stands behind us.

We all turn and look. The field hockey squad and the boys' and girls' soccer teams are filing into the gym. I spot Daniel as they fill the visitors' section.

"What are they doing here?" I ask.

"Sports events are always canceled or postponed when there's lightning," Sandy informs us.

Kayla moans. "Because thunderstorms are dangerous."

"I don't care why they're here," Liz says. "So long as they behave."

Alliyah bounds up to us. "Oh, yeah! Our bleachers are *full*!" She throws her arms overhead and points at the crowd. "What's the word, my peeps?" she shouts.

"Alliyah, sit down and shut it," Liz hisses. But it's too late.

"*Spooooooooon!*"

The word is the same. But the fans don't yell it like they did at the last game. Instead, they pitch their voices low and deep. They sound like a herd of cows mooing.

The Coyotes are on the court practicing their serves. A few look our way. A ball hurtles toward one of them. It hits her in the head. A teammate catches her as she stumbles. They both glare in our direction.

Their coach glares at us too. Coach Millburn's face is a mask of fury.

I grab Alliyah's arm. "You started this. You have to stop it. Now!"

Alliyah laughs. "How am I supposed to do that? And why would I? I like when they cheer for me!"

I stare at her. Then I yank my phone out of my backpack and speed-text Daniel.

Stop yelling Spoon! I write. **PLEASE!**

I send it, then spin to look at him.

He reads my message. Then he jumps up and faces the crowd. I can't hear everything he says, only the words *spoon* and *big trouble*. I know he's popular, but I'm still surprised when his teammates and the other students listen to him. Shushing sounds replace the mooing *spoon* cheer.

Daniel sits back down. He shoots me a thumbs-up and a smile.

"*Thank you*," I mouth to him. Then I turn back to the court—and jump because Coach Millburn is standing in front of me. Hands on her hips, she's frowning at my phone.

"Devices are not allowed during matches," she says.

"I-I know, Coach," I stammer. "I'm sorry. I just sent one text about . . . that." I gesture toward the stands.

Her eyes narrow. "Tell me you weren't behind that noise."

My jaw drops. "What? No! I was trying to stop it. Really!"

I hold up my phone. My text to Daniel is still on the screen. Her frown softens as she reads it.

"Ah, I see. Well, obviously, I'll overlook the no-phone rule. *This* time anyway." She smiles. "Thank you for taking charge of the situation before it got out of hand."

I blush at her praise. "No problem, Coach."

I slip my phone into the side pocket of my backpack. When I straighten, I catch Alliyah doing the same thing. She holds her hands up as if she's surrendering.

"Just making sure I'd silenced it before I 'take charge of the situation' on the court."

A whistle blows. Alliyah grins at me, then joins the other starters.

We have the ball first. Alliyah heads to the end line. She looks toward the ref for the signal to serve. Her gaze doesn't stop on him though. She keeps turning her head until she's looking at the stands.

Puzzled, I look there too.

Rochelle and other field hockey players are returning from the concession stand. They have bowls of chili. Two are also holding fistfuls of something white. Napkins, I think, because they pass them out to their teammates and all the soccer players.

Which is weird because those players don't have any food or drinks. So why would they need napkins?

I'm still trying to understand what I'm seeing when the

ref blows his whistle. The second he does, the fans move their hands in front of their faces. Each is holding one of the white things.

I suck in my breath. The white things aren't napkins.

They're plastic spoons.

CHAPTER 14

Lightning flashes in the windows again. A boom of thunder follows it. On the court, Kayla flinches.

And Alliyah looks at the fans and smirks knowingly. Her eyes gleam.

A shock runs through me. But it has nothing to do with the storm.

She texted them, I think, remembering her slipping her phone away. *When I shut down their yells, she told them to hold up spoons.*

I can't prove it. Not unless I see the text. Alliyah would never show me her phone. And I won't sneak it out of her backpack. That would cross a line.

If not Alliyah, then the person who got the text. Rochelle, maybe? She passed out some of the spoons, and Alliyah called her her BFF.

But why would Rochelle share Alliyah's text with me? And

even if she did . . . I slump forward with my elbows on my knees. *What would I do with it?*

I look to Coach Millburn, willing her to turn to the stands and see what's happening. But she doesn't because our fans aren't yelling or chanting or stomping their feet. They're just sitting with spoons in their hands. Showing their support for us.

No, not for us. For Alliyah.

Who tosses the ball in the air and crushes the first serve of the game. It's an ace. She aces the Coyotes on the second serve too. When they finally send the ball back over the net on the next one, she takes charge.

"Liz, it's yours!" She sprints to the right front corner of the net. Then yells, "Here-here-here-here-here!"

Thump! Liz bumps the ball to her.

"Sandy!" Alliyah cries. She flicks the ball to our outside hitter. Sandy times her approach perfectly. Three steps, a jump, and a booming hit. The ball rockets straight down to an empty spot on the Coyotes' side.

Lynx 3, Coyotes 0.

A Coyote player retrieves the ball. Grinning, Alliyah holds up her hands to catch it. Instead of lobbing it to her, the Coyote slowly rolls it under the net. Alliyah makes a face and scoops it up. As she jogs to the end line, she points a finger at our stands.

The subs and I look behind us at our fans. No one says a word. But those who have spoons wave them wildly.

Daniel is one of them.

I blink in surprise. Then I twist back around. Heat rides up my face. I don't know why I feel so betrayed. It's not like Daniel and I are going out. But seeing him with a spoon is still a punch to the gut.

I stare at the players on the court. But I don't follow the action. I don't know what the score is. And I don't hear Coach Millburn calling my name.

It takes Jill grabbing my arm to bring me back. "Earth to Macy! Come on, we're getting into the game! Let's go!"

She tugs me to the substitution area. Heather follows. Jill nudges me as Alliyah, Liz, and Jessie come to change places with us.

"You all right?" she asks. "You looked pretty zoned out."

"Yeah, I'm fine," I say.

Alliyah overhears. Instead of just touching my palm with hers, she grips my hand and pulls me close. "You better be all right," she whispers through a big smile. "I don't need you to blow our lead." Still smiling, she lets go.

I stare after her, speechless.

The ref taps my shoulder. "Miss? You're all set."

"Oh. Right. Thanks." I hurry onto the court and take my position.

"What are you doing?" Sandy hisses. "You're serving!"

"I am? I mean, yeah, I am!"

I look around for the ball. The same Coyote who slow-rolled it to Alliyah slow-rolls it to me. When I move to pick it up, I accidentally kick it.

The Coyotes snicker. So do their hometown fans. Completely flustered, I chase the ball, then carry it to the end line. I glance at the scoreboard. We're only up by three points, 13–10.

The ref signals for me to serve. Just as I toss the ball,

lightning flares. It blinds me for a second. Somehow, I power the ball over the net. But that's the only good thing I do while I'm on the court.

Tweet! I get whistled for a double hit, meaning my hands don't touch the ball at the same time when I set.

Tweet! My foot slips under the net onto the Coyotes' side, another foul.

Tweet! My hand brushes the top of the net when I try to tip the ball.

As my mistakes grow, my self-confidence tanks. Our lead shrinks. After what feels like forever, Alliyah comes back in for me.

She doesn't grip my hand this time. She just glares at me as we change places.

I keep my eyes on the floor as I head to the bench. Coach Millburn stops me.

"Macy," she says quietly. "You're a little off your game right now. But I know you're a good player. So take a deep breath. Don't let a few mistakes get you down. Okay?"

"Okay," I mumble.

My teammates look up as I pass them. A few hold out their hands. I tap their fingertips without any enthusiasm. Then I slump at the end of the bench.

Liz scoots close to me. She doesn't say anything. Just leans against me for a few seconds before straightening. That reassurance comforts me more than Coach Millburn's kind words.

The first game of the match ends a short while later. We win, but just barely, with a score of 25–21.

I start the second game. As I trot onto the court, someone in the stands yells, "Go get 'em, Macy!"

For a split second, I think it's Daniel. But when I glance up, I'm surprised to see my father smiling and clapping for me. He and Mom don't make many of my games because of work. I wish they'd missed this one too.

And Daniel? He and the players of the other Lynx teams are filing out of the bleachers. The storm has passed, so their games are back on.

Daniel looks my way as he goes by. He's still holding his spoon. He looks at it, then shakes his head and starts to mouth something to me. What, I don't know. His teammates get in the way.

Then a whistle shrieks. The Coyote player gets ready to serve.

I try to put Daniel out of my mind. To put the sea of plastic spoons out of it too. To focus on the game.

I try. But I fail.

CHAPTER 15

I don't like being in a funk. It doesn't feel good. But I can't snap out of it. And the deeper I sink, the sloppier my play gets.

I'm called for more double hits. I'm out of position and have to lunge for the ball. My passes are too low, too high, or too far. I run into my teammates when they try to help me. My mistakes make it impossible for us to get into a rhythm.

Even worse? The Coyotes know I'm the weak link. They target me with quick tips and hard hits. When Alliyah subs in, we trail 13–6.

Liz flashes me a smile of support. But it's weak and fades quickly.

"Show those claws, Lynx!" Alliyah cries.

She curls her fingers and growls as she jogs to the end line. Her serve rockets over the net. It looks like a line drive. But before it drops, it curves. The Coyote libero can't reach it. It hits the floor.

"Awwwwww—Ace!" our players yell. Then they make Lynx claws.

Those claws become their good luck charm. They show them before every serve. After every point we add to our side of the scoreboard. During time-outs.

I watch most of the action from the sidelines. More a spectator than a player. I sub in only so Alliyah can get a rest. Not that she needs one. Her energy is off the charts. With her playing, we slowly close the gap in the score.

But it's too little, too late. Final score: Coyotes 25, Lynx 20.

"Okay, we're tied at a game each," Coach Millburn says in our huddle. "We still have three games to play. Win two, and we win the match. So go out there and show them what you've got!"

Our starters make Lynx claws as they trot onto the court. But the momentum is on the Coyotes' side. And they ride it all the way to a second win.

We're down, but not out. We battle for every point in game four. So do the Coyotes. The lead seesaws back and forth. Lynx 5, Coyotes 4. Coyotes 8, Lynx 7. Lynx 12, Coyotes 10.

I sub into the game then. I'm tense when I swap places with Alliyah. I look to Jill for support as I get ready to serve. But she's hunched over in ready position and doesn't meet my eyes. Kayla shifts from foot to foot at the net. On the sidelines, Liz blows out a long, tired breath.

Only Coach Millburn claps for me. "Fire it up, Macy!"

I nod and take the ball to the endline. *Bring it*, I tell myself. *Your teammates need a boost.*

I find the spot where I want my serve to land. Then I throw the ball high overhead. One step, two steps, jump, swing, and hit! I put everything I have into my serve.

And it works! The ball soars over the net. It's heading right where I want it to go. I watch it as I charge to the setter's spot. I raise my arm. Open my mouth to call for the pass.

The ref blows his whistle. All the players freeze, then

look at him. He's pointing to the line judge on our side. Her flag is in the air. She's pointing at the end line. It's the signal for a service fault.

My heart drops into my stomach. I stepped on the line. My serve didn't help us. It hurt us. The point goes to the Coyotes.

I glance at Jill again. I need her to flash me the flush sign. But she's scrubbing her face with her hands. When she drops them, her lips are pinched. She looks miserable.

If she is, it's because of me.

I play a few more points. I don't mess up again. But I don't help much either.

When I come out of the game, the score is tied at 15 each. Coach Millburn calls a time-out. "Just ten more points, Lynx. That's all we need. And I know you can get them!"

We do get them. But so do the Coyotes. Games must be won by a two-point lead. So, at 25–25, the fight continues.

Coach Millburn takes another time-out. She urges us not to give up. To focus and to be the players she knows we are. Then she sends the starters back onto the court.

Behind us, our parents stand and cheer. So do our JV players, who finished their match half an hour earlier. They're loud. But they're outnumbered by the Coyotes' fans. When their team takes their positions, we're hit by a wall of sound.

They quiet down when their best server steps to the end line . . . then erupt again when she blasts the ball over the net.

Alliyah's shrill cries of "Here-here-here-here-here!" cut through the noise. Emma bumps a pass to her. Alliyah raises both hands. Drops one as she jumps to meet the ball.

"Tip! Tip!" the Coyotes shout.

I zero in on Alliyah's hand. Her fingers are aimed forward. *She's going to send it straight down*, I think.

The Coyote closest to the ball must think so too. She slides down low, arms out and ready.

The ball doesn't come to her. At the last second, Alliyah twists her wrist to the side. She flicks the ball away from the Coyote.

Another Coyote dives for it. My jaw drops. She gets her hand under it!

Everything seems to go in slow motion then. The ball bounces off the back of the Coyote's hand. It sails up high enough for her teammate to reach. She hits it over the net.

Kayla is right there. Arms high, she leaps and connects with the ball. I'm already out of my seat. It's going to be our point!

Except it isn't. The ball doesn't land on the Coyotes' side of the net. It lands on ours and rolls away.

The Coyotes' fans explode with roars, cheers, and foot stomps. Kayla crumples in on herself. Liz, Emma, Sandy, and Jessie rush to comfort her. Alliyah stares at them, then picks up the ball and hurls it to the Coyotes' server.

One serve later, our undefeated season comes to an end.

CHAPTER 16

"Man, it stinks that you guys lost." That's how Cam greets me at the salon the next morning.

Bette gives me a sympathetic hug. "How are you and your teammates doing?"

I shrug. "Okay, I guess."

The truth is, we aren't okay. The bus ride home was horrible. Coach Millburn told us not to dwell on the loss. "It's a three-day weekend, so use that time to relax," she said. "We'll focus on the next match at practice Monday morning."

She didn't say anything to us about the spoons. Maybe she was too focused on the match to notice what was going on behind her.

Sandy said a few words to us on the bus too. But Liz just stared out the window. Jill ripped off her jersey, pulled on her sweatshirt, and sat with her head tipped back, eyes closed. And Kayla flat-out refused to let anyone near her.

Back home, I tried calling Marie. It went right to her voicemail. I didn't have the energy to text or try again later.

And now I'm here at the salon. Saturdays mean lots of walk-ins. Three of the stylists are away for the long weekend. So Cam, Bette, and a new stylist, Rita, are super busy. I help out as best I can.

I'm bringing Rita some clean towels when Marco and a few boys burst through the door.

"Spoon!" Marco yells.

"Five!" the boys behind him cry. "Four!"

Startled, I drop the towels. Without even thinking, I race for my backpack.

"Three!" the boys shout. "Two!"

I race back. Breathing hard, I shove Mini Macy under their noses.

"Aww." They hustle out, disappointed.

"I'll get you next time," Marco calls over his shoulder.

The bell over the door jingles when it shuts behind him. I stash my spoon in my apron pocket and turn.

The stylists and their customers are staring at me. Bette and Cam do not look happy. And Rita looks terrified. She drops the scissors she's holding. They land on the towels by her chair. Eyes wide, she whispers, "I could have cut Mrs. Marsh with those."

Her customer jumps out of the chair. Her hair is dripping wet. "I'm going to skip the haircut for today," Mrs. Marsh says. She pulls off the nylon cape, grabs her purse, and hurries out the door.

"Macy." Bette's voice is cold. She sets her hairbrush aside and crooks a finger at me.

I follow her to the back room. "I'm so sorry, Bette! I—"

She holds up a hand to stop me. "I don't know what that was all about. But I don't want it to ever happen again. Rita is right. One wrong move, and she could have hurt her client. Now Mrs. Marsh will never come back. And she'll tell others, which means we'll lose customers."

I hang my head. "I'll pay for Mrs. Marsh's haircut. And I'll send a text. Make sure no one else comes in."

Bette nods curtly and returns to her client.

I get out my phone and text the volleyball team.

Spread the word: No Spoon where people work!

I hesitate, then text Daniel too. When it sends, I take Mini Macy out of my pocket.

I should throw it away. Snap it in half. Just stop playing Spoon.

My phone pings. It's a text from Jill. **What happened?**

Marco and his buddies happened. At the salon.

She replies with a furious-face emoji. **I'd snap Marco's spoon if I was still in the game! But I know you'll do it for me.**

There's another ping, this time with a text from Daniel. All it says is **K**.

I stare at that letter. Then I slowly slip my phone back into my backpack. I think about tossing Mini Macy again. But then I imagine how gleeful Alliyah will be to have me out of the game. I slip the spoon next to my phone and get back to work.

The hours tick by slowly. Customers come and go. No one else from school comes in. I work the register, stock the shelves, and move laundry from the washer to the dryer. And I apologize to the stylists over and over. At closing time, I refuse their tip money. But Bette insists, and so does Cam.

Before she leaves, Rita hands me a few bills too. After she's gone, I put the money in an envelope with her name on it and leave it in her work cubby.

Cam sees me do it. He nods his approval. He and I are closing up. When Bette heads out, he asks what she didn't. "What the heck is Spoon?"

I sigh and tell him.

"Hang on," he says. "That girl I gave pink stripes is the one who started it?" He shakes his head. "Yeah, she's trouble."

"Why do you say that?" I ask, curious.

"Three reasons." He holds up his index finger. A slim silver ring he wears winks in the light. "One, she tattled on you about the car ride. Which I know she must have talked you into giving her in the first place. You would *never* risk losing your license." He adds a second finger. "Two, she talked you into paying for her stripes."

When I start to protest, he shushes me. "Don't interrupt. Three." A third finger joins the other two. "You think she accidentally switched your ten-dollar bill with her one. I *know* she pocketed your ten and left me the one on purpose."

I blink. "How do you know that?"

He points to a dark bulb above the register. "Security camera, darling girl. You looked so bummed out when you left last week, I took a peek at the footage. I saw you pay with your tip money. Saw her swap the ten and the one too. I can show you the video if you want."

"No, I—that's—wow."

I sink into a chair. I'm not making sense. But he nods like he understands completely.

He sits in another chair and turns toward me. His face is serious. "I can't tell you what to do with this info, Macy. But I can tell you that Alliyah is banned from this salon for life. Because like I said . . . that girl is trouble."

CHAPTER 17

My parents aren't around when I get home. According to Mom's text, they went leaf-peeping in the mountains and are eating at a diner. She Venmos me money for pizza. But I can't eat. My mind and my stomach are churning with what Cam told me.

I try calling Marie. It goes to voicemail. This time, I leave a message asking her to get back to me. Then I take a long shower and crawl into bed with my laptop.

Sunlight on my face wakes me up in the morning. My head feels clearer, but I still don't know what to do about Alliyah.

I have made one decision though: I'm going to come clean to my parents about giving Alliyah a ride. I'll get in trouble, but anything is better than letting Alliyah hold that over me for one more minute.

But my folks are still asleep. Marie hasn't called back.

I think about what Cam said, about Alliyah being trouble. And I realize at least one other person needs to know what's been going on.

I video call Jill.

"Mmmmm?" She's groggy and has a bad case of bedhead. I love that she answered anyway.

"Sorry to wake you up," I say. "But I have something to tell you."

She sits up. "Is it Marco again? If so, I'll handle him." She growls and shakes her fist.

"Marco isn't the problem. Not this time, anyway. I am."

I tell her everything. As in *everything*. With each incident I unload, a weight lifts off my shoulders. It feels good to finally get this off my chest.

Jill's so outraged she can't speak for a full ten seconds. Then she says, "You were foolish to risk your license for Alliyah."

I scrub my face with my hands. "You're right."

"No duh. Now, about Alliyah using the car ride to get you to pay for her stripes . . . got proof?"

I smile. Jill loves police and detective shows. *Got proof* is her favorite catchphrase. "Besides the salon footage? No."

She frowns. "I bet that footage doesn't have sound. Which means Alliyah could just say you offered to pay. And that Cam's tip was a mix-up. As for blackmailing you—"

"Whoa!" I interrupt her. "I never said anything about blackmail!"

She makes a face. "What else do you call it when someone bullies money out of you the way she did?"

I groan and flop back against my pillow.

Jill takes pity on me. "Right. Let's skip over the B-word and focus on how to get Alliyah benched and you back in the starting lineup."

I shake my head. "No. I can't do that to the team."

"Exsqueeze me?"

I roll my eyes. "Come on, Jill. We both know Alliyah is better than me. By a lot." When she frowns, I throw her favorite phrase back at her. "I got proof. I was awful against the Coyotes. I basically cost us the match!"

Jill sputters. "You think *you* played bad? What about me? What about Liz? And Kayla?"

I frown. "What about you? And them?"

"Dude, I had a screaming headache from that rancid bathroom soap. Liz was so tired her eyeballs were rolling around in her head. And Kayla was nearly having a panic attack because of the thunderstorm. None of us played our best that match. So, the better team won."

I open my mouth to protest. Close it again.

"No one player should be blamed for a loss," I finally murmur. "And no one player should get credit for a win."

"That sounds familiar. Who said it?"

I smile. "Marie."

"I knew I'd heard you say it before. It's so good, we should put it on a T-shirt."

"Yeah." My smile fades. "If only there was a T-shirt that could help me decide what to do about Alliyah."

"Actually, there is." Jill lays her phone on the bed. For a few moments, I have a great view of her ceiling. Then she returns. She's changed out of her pj top and is wearing a gray tee. On it are the words *Listen to your gut*.

She poses like a model. "Like it? My mom got it at a yoga thing. It's all about trusting your inner voice or whatever."

"Not the rumbles my stomach makes when I'm hungry?" I joke.

"You should always listen to those," she says seriously. "Anyway, close your eyes. Think about Alliyah. About how she's been treating you. And about what might happen if you speak up. Then tell me what your gut says to do." She waves a hand. "Go on, now. Shut your peepers."

Feeling a little silly, I close my eyes. I think about Alliyah. *Really* think. I think about Marie's advice to put team and teammates first too. And I wonder if it makes sense to follow that advice when the teammate is Alliyah. When I open my eyes, I know what I want to do.

"I'm going to talk to Rochelle about the Coyotes' match," I say. "I'll ask if Alliyah texted her to do the spoon thing. If she has the text, I'll see if she'll share it with me."

"And if she wasn't the one or refuses to share?"

"If Rochelle is a dead end, then I switch to beating Alliyah at Spoon. Actually," I add, smiling, "I'll do that anyway."

Before she can reply, my phone dings with an incoming call. I blink when I see the name. "Um, it's Daniel."

"Oooooo!" she singsongs. Then she grimaces. "Sorry, that sounded too much like *spooooon*."

She hangs up. I wait a beat. I'm still hurt by what Daniel did at the match. And by his last text. But I'm curious too. So, I accept the call.

"Hello?" My voice is guarded.

I hear Daniel clear his throat. "Oh. Uh, hi, Macy. You answered."

"Isn't that what I'm supposed to do when my phone rings?" I say coolly.

"Yeah. It's just . . . it rang long enough I thought you were ignoring me."

"Well, I'm not."

There's a long pause. Then we both talk at the same time.

"Why did you want us to wave spoons at your match?" he says.

"Why did you wave a spoon at my match?" I blurt. Then his words filter into my brain. "Hold up. Why do you think I was behind that spoon thing?"

Daniel's answer should shock me. But it doesn't.

"Alliyah said you asked her to text Rochelle about it," he says. "And then Rochelle took it from there."

CHAPTER 18

Daniel doesn't have the text Alliyah sent to Rochelle.

"I should have known you weren't behind it though," he says. "I mean, you had me stand up in front of everyone and get them to stop yelling *spoon*."

"I know. That was amazing, by the way."

He chuckles. The sound is warm and rich, like hot chocolate. "Thanks. Gotta admit, I was pretty excited when they all listened to me. That was why I was so confused when someone shoved an actual spoon in my hand and said you wanted me to wave it."

"That wasn't my idea, I promise," I insist. "And for the record, I hated it. Almost as much as that *K* you texted."

"I only sent that because I thought you were jerking me around!" He makes his deep voice high. "'Tell them to stop, Daniel.' 'No, take this spoon, Daniel, and hold it in the air!' '*OMG*, Daniel, tell Marco to get out of my face with his spoon!'"

I'm laughing so hard I can barely speak. "I do *not* sound like that," I finally say. "But I get why you were mad."

"I'm over it now. Are you over being mad at me?"

"Yeah."

The vibe between us shifts then. I'm glad it's a regular phone call, not a video chat. Not because my bedhead is even worse than Jill's, though it is. I'm blushing so hard my face feels like it's on fire.

"I miss hanging out with you like we did this summer," he says.

"Me too."

"We should start hanging out more."

I switch my phone to my other ear. My heart is singing. "We should."

"Like, *just* you and me. No little campers running around and bothering us."

"That sounds good." Then I take a big leap. "How about

tomorrow? We have volleyball practice in the morning, even though there's no school."

"We have soccer practice then too. Want to go to that burger place afterward?"

My smile is so wide it almost splits my face. "My gut is telling me to say yes."

"Because it likes burgers?"

"Sure. Let's go with that."

We hang up a few minutes later. Talking with Jill and Daniel has helped me feel a lot better. I'm not sure my next conversation is going to be as nice.

I find my parents in the kitchen and tell them about Alliyah and the car ride. They're not angry, but they're disappointed. They take away my car privileges for two weeks, which is why Mom drives me to the high school gym the next morning.

"Is Daniel giving you a ride home after your lunch?" she asks as I get out of the car.

I roll my eyes. "Yes, Mother. He's not going to leave me

stranded." Then I lean in. "But you're around if it doesn't go well, right?"

She smiles. "Of course. But it will."

In the locker room, I keep one eye peeled for Alliyah and one hand on Mini Macy. I look for Rochelle too. But the field hockey team starts practice later than us.

I change into my volleyball gear, fold my leggings neatly, and hang my hoodie on the hook. I slip my backpack in and put Mini Macy in my hoodie pouch. Then I lock my locker and head into the gym.

"All right, Lynx," Coach Millburn calls. "We'll begin with hitting lines. Then we'll scrimmage."

Alliyah starts for the court. Then she stops. "Coach, I need to use the bathroom."

"Make it quick," Coach says. "Macy, you're up."

I jog to the setter's spot by the net. The hitters form a line on the left side of the court. Liz, Jill, and Emma go to the back row. Coach Millburn wheels the ball cart to the center. "Here we go!"

She tosses a ball to Liz. Liz bumps it to me, then races

to the other side of the court. I set it to Sandy. Sandy runs up and hits it over the net. Liz fetches the ball, tosses it in the cart, and returns to the back row.

Coach Millburn is already tossing the next ball to Jill. I fall into the smooth rhythm of toss, bump, set, hit, fetch, repeat. I don't notice how long we've been doing it until Coach says, "Sandy, go check on Alliyah."

"No need!" Alliyah comes out of the locker room. Her face looks flushed. But she's grinning. "Sorry. I, um . . ." She waves vaguely at her lower body.

Coach Millburn holds up her hands. "Understood."

Alliyah takes my spot without being told. I stand back until it's time to swap in. The hitters switch to the right side of the court.

"Looking good, Macy!" Coach Millburn calls when I back set to Jessie.

I glow inside. I know I'm playing better than I did on Friday. Better than I have since the game against the Condors, too, when I twisted my ankle and lost my starter's spot to Alliyah.

Is she better than me? Yes. *But maybe not that much better*, I think.

We take a water break after hitting lines, then finish practice with a light scrimmage. It's competitive but fun, the way volleyball should be. At the end, we huddle up with our hands in the middle. "One, two, three—LYNX!" we shout.

I'm the first one in the locker room. Daniel and I are meeting outside in ten minutes. I change out of my sweaty volleyball gear. I do a quick hair and makeup fix, then shove everything into my backpack and head outside.

My phone buzzes. It's Daniel. **See you in 5!**

I text back a thumbs-up emoji and slip my phone back into my pocket. That's when I realize that the pocket is empty. No Mini Macy. I search my backpack. Nothing.

At that moment, a car slowly rolls up. Thinking it's Daniel, I move toward it.

Sandy's behind the wheel. She's looking at me and laughing.

"Hi?" I say uncertainly.

Suddenly, Alliyah pops up in the passenger seat. She has something in her hand. It's my spoon.

"Hey!" I cry. I grab the car handle and try to open the door. It's locked.

Grinning, Alliyah holds Mini Macy with two hands and snaps it in two. She waves the pieces at me, grinning even wider. "I beat you," she crows. "I beat you!"

CHAPTER 19

The car roars away. I stand there, stunned.

I don't care that I'm out of the game. I truly don't. It's *how* I got knocked out that has me speechless.

My spoon was in my hoodie pocket. My hoodie was locked in my locker. There's only one way it could have ended up in Alliyah's hands.

"What was that all about?" Daniel is walking toward me. When he sees my face, he picks up his pace. "Seriously, Macy, what's going on?"

"I was robbed, that's what." I outline what happened.

His eyes widen. "She broke into your locker? We have to tell someone!"

I shake my head. "I can't prove it. She'll just say she found it on the floor or make some other excuse."

"There must be something we can do."

"Yeah." I nod, taking a deep breath. I need to think

about how to handle what just happened. But first . . .

"We can get burgers."

The restaurant is packed. We try to talk. It's so noisy we can't hear each other. Daniel takes out his phone. He sends me a text.

Next time, let's pick a quieter place!

Wanna get our food to go? I reply.

Absolutely!

Twenty minutes later, we're sitting in his car in a park by a lake. We share a huge order of fries and tear into our burgers. He tells me a funny story about when he was eight and his dad signed him up for soccer instead of football. "It was an honest mistake. He's from Brazil. Soccer is called football there. I was so mad. I really wanted to wear a helmet!"

I'm still laughing when he drops me off at home. A few minutes later, my phone buzzes. I hope it's him.

It's a message from a number I don't recognize. There's no text, just a video. The image beneath the Play arrow is of our locker room.

Puzzled, I click the arrow. The video bounces around, then zooms in on a girl standing in front of my locker. It's Alliyah. She looks right, then left, then spins my combination and opens the door. She grabs my backpack and rummages around inside it. She takes out my phone. Runs her thumb over the screen, then makes a face and puts it back. Then she pulls out my hoodie.

I shiver. I'm wearing that same hoodie right now.

She shakes it out. Then she smiles and reaches into the pocket. Out comes Mini Macy. She smiles even wider than before.

The video ends there. I stare at the frozen image of Alliyah holding Mini Macy and smiling. Then I grit my teeth and shake my head.

Enough is enough. I type a short text.

Hey Coach, it's Macy. Please look at this. And please meet with me before school tomorrow morning. Thank you.

I take a deep breath, attach the video, and hit send. Then I open my group chat with Liz and Jill and send them the video too. I shower. When I get out, my phone is pinging and buzzing like a pinball machine. I snatch it up. And almost drop it on the bathroom floor.

I didn't send the video to just Liz and Jill. I sent it to the whole varsity volleyball team. Including Alliyah, whose texts are blowing up my screen.

Stab me in the back, why don't you, Macy?

She's obviously pissed because I'm a better player!

What kind of creeper takes secret videos of teammates?

Spoon rules allow you to steal, remember? So NBD!

It's a big deal to me though. I'm about to text as much when a new message appears. It's from Coach Millburn.

Come to my office at 7, it says.

I reply that I'll be there.

Dad drops me off at school a few minutes before seven the next morning.

Coach Millburn is waiting for me in her office. I take a seat. And I tell her everything that Alliyah has said and done since the Condors' match. I also tell her how I disobeyed the junior driver's license rules by driving Alliyah home. How I knew I'd broken the Code and would understand if she benched me because of it.

When I'm done, she drums her fingers on her desk and studies me for a long moment. When she finally speaks, her question surprises me. "Why did you stay quiet about Alliyah for so long, Macy?"

"I didn't want to get her in trouble," I say. "I didn't think that would be fair to the team. I believed our best chance of getting to the playoffs and winning the championship was with her on the court."

"And now?"

I lift my chin. "Alliyah is a better player than me. But I don't think she's what's best for the team. And for what it's worth," I add, "I'm really sorry I kept playing Spoon. Especially when you asked us not to."

The coach runs her hand through her hair. "I should have tried to shut down that game after the Lions' match."

I shift in my seat. "So, what happens now?"

"Now I have a hard talk with Alliyah. As for you—"

I hold my breath.

"I'll see you at practice this afternoon."

I can't believe it. I jump up, thank her, and leave in a happy daze.

Alliyah is waiting outside in the hall. She gives me a dirty look before disappearing into Coach's office. I don't stick around.

I'm at my locker getting my things for my first period class when she charges up.

"Thanks a lot," she yells. "I just got benched for three days!"

I slam my locker door and face her. "And?"

"And it's your fault!"

"No." I step closer to her. "You broke into my locker."

Alliyah throws her hands in the air. "Because we were playing a game! That's what you should have told Coach. Instead, you threw me under the bus."

Silence has fallen over the crowded hallway. A group of

students has their phones aimed at us. I shake my head. "I'm done talking about this now."

Alliyah scoffs. "Let's talk at practice then. Oh no, wait, we can't! Because of you, I'm not allowed to be there!"

She spins on her heel and stalks away.

CHAPTER 20

The volleyball section of the locker room is like a graveyard. I feel everyone's eyes on my back as I get changed. I startle when someone taps me on the shoulder.

"Can we talk?" Sandy asks. I brace myself and turn. To my surprise, the rest of the team has gathered behind her.

"I want to apologize," Sandy says. "Until I saw the video, I had no idea Alliyah stole your spoon. She told me she found it on the floor."

"Not what happened," I say stiffly. "Obviously."

"Yeah." Sandy bites her lip. "Also, as your co-captain, I should have checked in with you after Alliyah took over your spot. It was a mistake not to. I'm sorry."

I relax a little. "It's okay. Liz made sure I was good."

Sandy nods, then glances at the others.

Kayla clears her throat. "Alliyah is a really good setter."

A few players murmur in surprise at her praise. Kayla

shushes them. "I'm not finished. Macy, you knew she'd be benched if Coach found out she stole your spoon. But you sent the video anyway. Not to stick it to Alliyah, but because it was the right thing to do. That took guts." She smiles at me. "I like guts."

Jill claps me on the back. "You all seem to forget that we were undefeated when Macy was in the starting lineup. And we'll win the rest of our matches with her back in it."

"That's right." Liz puts her hand out. The others follow. Grinning, I stack mine on top. "One, two, three—"

"LYNX!" we bellow.

Coach Millburn calls me to her office then. The JV setter is with her. "I've added Felicity to our roster," Coach tells me. "She'll be your backup for the next few days."

I smile at the sophomore. "I've been watching you play. You've got good hands."

The other players greet Felicity just as warmly. She's quiet but jumps right into everything we do. I think she'll fit in just fine.

Practice goes well. My teammates and I fall easily into

our old rhythm. We move like a well-oiled machine. Like a team. The locker room mood afterward is lighter and happier. And no one yells *spoon*.

Then Emma groans. "Oh, man. Alliyah was supposed to host our team get-together tonight."

"Shoot," Sandy says. "Can someone else do it?"

When no one volunteers, I text my folks and ask if we can. "Dad is running an online seminar and needs quiet tonight. But how about after we beat the Falcons tomorrow? We can be as loud as we want then."

Everyone gives the idea a big thumbs-up. I'm looking forward to the fun. Then Mother Nature screws up my plans.

"Don't get me wrong. I like snow." I'm video chatting with Jill by my window Wednesday morning. Outside, heavy flakes are falling steadily. Five inches of snow already cover the ground. "I'm a big fan of snow days too. But I wanted to play volleyball today!"

"Speaking of volleyball, does today count as Alliyah's

first suspension day? Or does that start tomorrow now instead?"

I blink. "I don't know. But if it starts tomorrow, it will go through Monday. Right?"

"I guess."

We play the Jaguars on Monday. Can we beat them without Alliyah?

I erase the thought as soon as it crosses my mind. Alliyah is a better player than me. But I'm a good setter too. More importantly, I'm a better teammate. I don't say that to Jill. I don't have to because she already knows it.

Jill yawns and snuggles deeper into her covers. "Time to hibernate. Wake me in the spring." We sign off.

Daniel calls a while later. I ask him what the soccer team does when it snows. "Pray we don't have to shovel the field," he answers.

Liz checks in too. **I finished my essay!!!**

I reply with every celebration emoji and GIF I can find.

She sends back a smiley face and a question: **Still want to have the team get-together tonight?**

I check my weather app. It's supposed to stop snowing soon. But to be safe, I answer, **TBD L8R.**

The app proves to be right. By early afternoon, the snow eases up, then ends. The clouds disappear. The sun shines in the blue sky. People fire up their snowblowers. Plows clear the roads.

So, I send a group text: **The team hangout is still on!**

Within minutes, everyone responds that they're coming. Everyone except Alliyah.

My teammates show up dressed for snow. We make snow volleyball players in the backyard. Then someone throws a snowball. A full-on snowball fight erupts. We're all laughing and chasing each other when Alliyah appears. The fight grinds to a halt.

"I thought it was my turn to host." She sneers at me. "Guess you couldn't wait to take that away from me too."

"Whoa, Alliyah," Sandy says. "That's a little harsh."

"Harsh?" Alliyah echoes. "Being suspended for playing Spoon is harsh. So is being secretly videoed by a teammate! Which one of you took it?"

"None of us," I answer. "We were on the court while you were . . ." I imitate the way she waved at her lower body that morning.

Alliyah looks unconvinced. "Fine, don't tell me. But I'll tell you all something instead." She draws herself up tall. "My suspension starts tomorrow. So, I can't play Monday. Which means the Lynx are going to lose."

She looks strangely triumphant. Like it's a victory for her that she's benched for the Jaguars' match.

I sigh. "You really don't get it, do you?"

"Don't get what?" she challenges.

"That volleyball is a team sport," I say. "That means no one player gets credit for a win."

"And no one player gets blamed for a loss," Jill adds.

Liz joins us. "We're supposed to work together. Build each other up, not knock each other down."

"And we're supposed to be able to count on our teammates," I put in. "To trust them one hundred percent."

I don't add that she's lost our trust. If she doesn't know that, then my telling her won't change it.

Alliyah glances around. Her face turns to stone. "Whatever." Then she spins on her heel and storms off.

For a second, none of us moves. Then Jill claps her hands together. "Well, that was a moment. Now, how about those snacks?"

The team hangout breaks up after the snacks are gone. I head to bed tired from playing in the snow. And happy knowing that my teammates have my back.

CHAPTER 21

The next day, we face the Falcons. They're a decent team. But they don't have Kayla's height or Liz's quickness. They don't have Emma's instincts or Sandy's and Jessie's power. They don't have subs who cheer for their starters and make a difference when they get into the game.

When I'm on the court, I help put those pieces together. Point by point, we cruise to victory in game one. Then in game two. When the final whistle blows, we've defeated the Falcons three games to none.

I head into the locker room feeling good about Monday's match against the Jaguars. When I open my locker, a note falls out. Puzzled, I pick it up.

Want to know who took the video? Meet me in the back corner of the parking lot after practice tomorrow, it says.

I look around. I think I know who left it.

My suspicions are confirmed when a girl approaches me in the parking lot the next afternoon.

"Rochelle." I hold up the scrap of paper. "You left this."

She shoves her hands deep into her jacket pockets. "Yeah."

"And you took the video," I say.

"Yeah," she says again. "I was in the bathroom when Alliyah came in. She looked sneaky. I know that look from when we were kids. It usually ended in trouble back then. So I hid behind the wall. When she went to your locker, I hit Record. And then I sent the video to you."

I don't ask her why she sent it anonymously. It doesn't matter now. Instead, I ask, "Did she text you before the Coyotes' game?"

Rochelle sighs. "She did, but she said you told her to. I thought that was weird. You wanting us to wave spoons around was, too, especially after your boyfriend told us to stop with the spoon stuff."

I blush at her calling Daniel my boyfriend. "I didn't ask her to send that text."

She nods. "Yeah, I figured that out later. Anyway, now you know everything. Except that I'm done being friends with Alliyah." She sighs again, then pulls out a set of car keys. "You need a ride?"

I'd texted Daniel earlier. He's waiting for me in his car. "Got one, thanks."

"That's good. Because I'm not allowed to drive anyone for a few more months."

I laugh. "Same. See you."

She gets in her car and drives off. Daniel pulls up a moment later. I smile and slip into the passenger seat. It feels good to be in his warm car. Even better to be in his warm car with him.

We go to a frozen yogurt shop. He pays. "You get the next one," he says when I protest.

We take our cups to a table. "Shoot, I forgot something," he says.

"What?"

He looks sheepish. "A spoon."

I crack up as he returns to the counter. I don't know

where this thing between us is going. But I sure like where it is right now.

The weekend flies. Work is fun—no Spoon interruptions this time—and my homework is light, so I have time to hang out with Liz and Jill on Sunday.

And then suddenly, it's Monday, and we have our match against the Jaguars.

The JV team plays first. Felicity sits with Liz, Jill, and me. "It's weird being here instead of on the court with them," she says.

I bump her gently. "Get used to it. I'm pretty sure you're coming with us to the playoffs. Cassie and Helen too." I point at the JV hitter and middle blocker.

"And then there's next season," Jill says. She jerks a thumb at Liz. "This babe will be in college—"

"If I get in," Liz interrupts.

"Please, girl. You will," Jill says. "But Macy and I will still be here." She nudges Felicity. "If you and your teammates vote right, we'll be your captains."

"Jill!" I cry. "You can't beg for votes."

She shrugs. "It's not begging. It's campaigning."

The JV team wins their match in record time. Liz claps her hands. "All right, Lynx! Way to get it!"

Mom and Dad surprise me by showing up for our match. And they bring someone with them . . . sort of.

"It's Marie!" Mom calls. She points her phone toward me. I can just barely make out my sister's face on the tiny screen. But I love that she's watching all the way from Denmark.

Daniel and the other soccer players have an away game. Rochelle said she and some of the field hockey players were planning to come watch after their practice.

I hope they can find seats. Our bleachers are packed. I wonder if Alliyah is in the crowd. If she is, I don't see her. I'm okay with her staying away. I'll see more than enough of her when her suspension is over.

Or not. After the scene she made at my house, it's hard to imagine her returning to the team.

It's her choice. I'll deal with whatever she decides.

The gym is decorated for Senior Night. Posters celebrating Sandy, Liz, and the other seniors cover the walls. Green-and-white fairy lights twinkle around the bleachers. Balloons of the same colors bob and float by the entrances.

Before warm-ups begin, each of the seniors is introduced. They walk with their parents to the center of the gym. They and their mothers each receive a single white rose.

It's awesome.

When the ceremony is over, the Jaguars warm up. I watch them for a few minutes.

The Jaguars' warm-up time ends. We race onto the court. Our fans go wild. They shout our seniors' names. It sounds so much sweeter than any yell of "Spoon!" I grin and add my voice to theirs. We run through our hitting lines. Then we practice our serves.

And then it's game time.

The Jaguars have the ball first. A hush falls over the gym when the ref blows her whistle. The server bounces the ball three times. Tosses it high. Jumps and slams it over the net.

Our side is already in motion.

"Here!" I cry as I dart to the right front corner.

Emma bumps it to me. I set to Sandy. She smacks it over. The Jaguars' defensive specialist sends it right back. Not on purpose, I think. At least, her setter looks angry at being robbed of the second touch.

Liz passes to me. "Jessie!" I shout. I back set, making sure both hands flick the ball at exactly the same moment. No double hits for me this game.

Jessie connects and powers the ball cross-court. It hits the floor close to the Jaguars' sideline. Is it over the line? Or inbounds?

I hold my breath as the assistant ref hesitates. Then she stabs both hands downward. It's in!

The Jaguars' coach throws his arms up and spins away. His tantrum doesn't change the call though.

It's our point. Our serve.

My serve.

I scoop up the ball. I hurry to my favorite spot behind the end line, turn back to the court, and wait.

The ref blows her whistle and signals for me to serve.

The gym goes completely silent. I bounce the ball in rhythm with my heartbeat. Once, twice, three times. I balance it in the palm of my left hand. One more beat. One deep inhale in. One long exhale out. I smile.

Then I flip the ball in the air, run forward, and fly.

ABOUT THE AUTHOR

Stephanie True Peters is a freelance children's book writer with a diverse portfolio of published works featuring princesses and swamp monsters, inspirational men and heroic dogs, sports of all sorts, and Greek mythology. An avid reader, workout enthusiast, animal lover, and firm believer that our words and actions matter, Stephanie lives in Mansfield, Massachusetts, with her husband, Dan, an aging cat, and two rabbits.

TURN THE PAGE TO DISCOVER MORE EXCITING HORIZON TITLES!

HORIZON

FIREBIRD CAGED

MAYA CHHABRA

Ashley didn't mean to get pregnant her senior year in high school. She didn't mean to scare her hardworking and financially struggling mom, or to hide the truth from her awkward ex, Danny. She also didn't mean to illegally take her well-off friend Madi's prescription Xanax to cope with the stress—and she definitely didn't mean to do it more than once.

When a doctor reports Ashley to the State of Wisconsin as a drug-addicted threat to her own unborn child, she is forcibly detained under the obscure and secretive Act 292 civil detention system for pregnant women, stranded in the county juvenile shelter home, and stigmatized by authorities who assign her fetus a lawyer but not her. It's a struggle for Ashley just to get medical care for the pregnancy supposedly being protected—never mind fighting for her own freedom and making sure her baby isn't taken away by social services after birth. Who's going to protect Ashley herself?

But Ashley is stronger than anyone knows, and she has allies on the outside who believe in her. This is a fight Ashley can win—but only if she stops drifting passively, starts believing in herself, and chooses not to give in to despair.

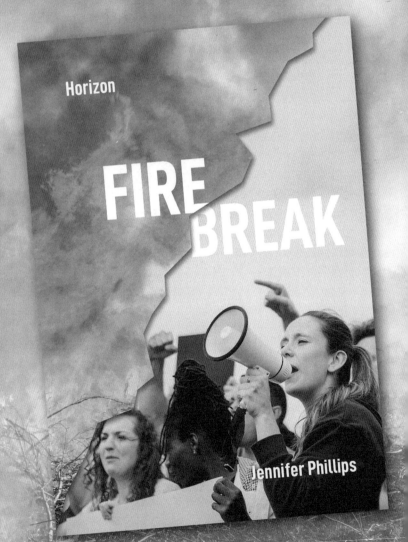

High school junior Alia is good at sports but struggles with schoolwork, hindered by her learning disabilities. The latest history assignment on genocide is just more homework to be endured. That's until a troubling conversation with her beloved grandmother reluctantly jolts Alia into action. Between the country's shifting mood toward the elderly and new government programs championed as practical ways to deal with a burgeoning elderly population, Alia fears that senior citizens are being targeted for something more ominous. To rally others and challenge the growing oppression, Alia will need to step up and speak out. But people tend to doubt Alia due to her learning difficulties. Can she get people to listen to her? More importantly, can she believe in herself?

Locked In Escape Rooms has a new owner. He's offering prize money for whoever can successfully escape the room. Four very different teenagers answer the call. Tony is a star athlete and honor-roll student. Bea has social anxiety and uses puzzles to tune out the noise. Anna is concerned about the rise in anti-Semitic attacks in her community. And Devin wants to hide that he's homeless and living in the mall. The four teens agree to work together, all seeking the prize money for their own reasons. But as the game begins, the escape room turns out to be stranger than expected, and they suspect someone might have ulterior motives in coming here. Can the teens overcome their prejudices and differences and trust one another in order to escape in time?

CHECK OUT OTHER HORIZON FICTION TITLES!

HORIZON

WALKING ON EGGSHELLS

JENNIFER PHILLIPS

After a first episode of psychosis lands him a stay in a psychiatric hospital, all sixteen-year-old Kai Lum wants to do is reclaim his life. But now that he's back home, everything is different. He has medications to take, his dad is always hovering, and everyone at school keeps staring at him. Kai's determined not to let any of that distract him from proving he can make it as a chef, though. He has his culinary arts program to focus on, and he won't let his diagnosis change his plans.

But finding his new normal is harder than Kai expects. His medications have side effects that he doesn't know how to control. His dad pushes him to accept more clinical help, even though Kai's not sure he wants—or needs—it. And Kai's best friends are ghosting him. On top of all of that, Kai isn't sure if the voices he's hearing are real or in his head.

Kai's life begins to spin out of control as he struggles to know who he can trust. With his health and dreams on the line, he has to decide whether he's willing to accept help in order to manage his newly diagnosed mental illness.